The Assassination Race

Secrets of The Afterlife Society

Ronnie Stich

ISBN: 0615814409
ISBN-13: 9780615814407

Thank you, Chris. You believed in me through the good times and the bad. Special thanks to Carla F. Sanchez, Bill Rattay, Chris, and my mother, Kathi, for taking the time to read my work before it was complete. Thanks to both Jonathan Cuellar and Julian Garcia for being friends for life. I love you both. Thanks to "Cadillac" Adam Balderas and to Rick Gomez of Rick Gomez Photography for the photo shoots and good memories. Susan Berilla, you passed away while I was bringing this book to life. I will always remember your laugh, and you will be missed.

Thanks to my two kids, Abby and Luke, for wanting to read this book even though I said they weren't old enough yet (Abby peeked anyway). Thank you to my friends that kept me going with their encouraging words while I wrote endlessly. When people believe in you, it shows. Thanks to the Misfits and Danzig for the great music while I wrote and while I was growing up back in the day. Thanks to the guys from "The World's Greatest Horror Rock Band," Calabrese, for keeping me going while I was writing. I would like to thank Paul Mancha, lead investigator and founder of the Silent Society of the Paranormal of Del Rio, Texas for being open-minded enough to do what he does and to include me in some of it along the way. Thanks to my Grandfather (because he is a wonderful and interesting man) and to my mother for both being great supporters of my writing. Without my mom, this book would not be read the way it was meant to be. And to my grandmother ... I love and miss you. You are my idea of strength and your words are always with me.

This work, I let sit for eight years and through three moves. It was an emotional challenge to bring it back into my life. To the people of Del Rio, Texas ... Thank you for the inspiration and kindness.

1

"Why are you looking at me like that?" she asked.

Edward was stunned. He shook uncontrollably as the gun in his hands teetered back and forth on the edge of being dropped several times.

"He's an asshole, Eddie." She lacked remorse or any emotion that would seem remotely appropriate. They were talking about murder. "You would be doing the citizens of Dallas a serious favor."

Somehow, he managed to gain enough control over himself to place the gun on top of the bar. He stood up, his eyes glazed over. "I'm leaving."

"No, you can't," she said. "You see, this is what I was talking about. Things are different now and it's my fault."

"You people are crazy," Edward said, staring into the crowded room like a zombie. Most of the people he could make out in the darkness stood clustered into small groups, each one of them engaged in conversation. Trays of hors d'oeuvres and wine floated around the dimly lit room. And not one of them seemed to have noticed that he had just been holding a gun.

"Actually, it's Gene's fault. I could have just taken you straight home if he hadn't pulled us over and said all that stuff about ... well, you heard him," Deidra corrected herself. She lifted the gun from the bar and turned in her seat to place it back into Edward's hands. He refused. He stepped away from her, flashing a look of terror. "I mean, he just blurts things out to anyone. He has no filter. The guy gets paid to cover things up for the government ... to keep things quiet. The other night, he was bragging about a hit he did to some guy in a bar. He tells him how he was paid for it with two stolen Dali paintings and a Picasso."

"I said I'm leaving," he added in clear protest. His heart rate felt like it had tripled.

"Look! Wolfman's here!" Deidra pointed across the room and waved. "Yes! I love that guy." She then laughed and placed the gun into her handbag, put the strap around her shoulder, and stepped closer to Edward. She moved in toward his ear and whispered, "They will kill you if you don't do it."

"Not if I get away first," he claimed.

"You can't get away. Don't be stupid, Eddie," she told him. "You've watched way too many movies. You won't win."

He contemplated his next move. If he pretended to go along with it, he could get the gun back from her and run for the exit. But if she was right, the weirdos surrounding them would somehow overtake him, probably slit his throat, and drink his blood in expensive snifters. Just out of the corner of his eye, he could see James Dean eating sushi with some guy dressed as a Mexican wrestler.

"How come no one ever comes to this thing as Marlon Brando? Did you ever see that old movie with the motorcycles? Do you know what I'm talking about?"

What am I doing here? They can't force me to kill someone, can they?

It was at that moment that Edward realized how different his evening would have been had he just—at some point in his overly boring life—taken the time to learn how to drive a car with a manual transmission. In fact, maybe he should have never contacted his old college pal Mike. He should have stayed in Austin instead of moving to Dallas and into Mike's apartment. He definitely shouldn't have accepted the job offer from Corpotex. Then, he wouldn't be standing in the middle of a group of secret society freaks that expected him to kill a crooked-as-fuck cop named Gene.

2

Edward's first day on the job went as typically as he thought it would. He listened in on a few sales calls to see exactly how things went and learned about the software he was supposed to sell in more detail. At lunch, Mike talked about boobs. Edward listened as Mike debated the pros and cons of dating a girl with breast implants while picking celery out of his so-called gourmet vegetable soup. After lunch, Edward locked himself out of his computer a few times because he forgot the new passwords he had created and had to wait hours for a tech support guy to save him. During the wait, he completed a crossword puzzle.

Close to 5 o'clock, Mike made his way down from his cushy office on the fourth floor to find Edward stuck in his cubicle on the third. While people were busy packing up their things to leave for the day, Edward was slumped over his desk, staring at the Internet. Mike approached him with a disappointed look on his face. "Hey man, I have to stay after for a few hours. I've been working on this report and …"

"So, should I wait around?" Edward asked. Carpooling to work with Mike would only be necessary until he could save up enough money to buy his own car.

"No. It'll take too long. There's a bus that goes by the apartment though," Mike suggested.

"What? I can't take the bus," he said with a look of dread on his face.

"Why not, Eddie?"

Edward cringed. "Don't call me 'Eddie,' Mike. It makes me violent," he joked.

"Just catch the bus. It's around the corner. Are you embarrassed or something?"

"Obviously."

Mike sighed and looked at his watch. "Look man, I gotta stay after. I'd offer you my car, but you can't drive standard ..."

"I know, but I just need 10 minutes to learn," Edward confessed, cutting Mike's words short with a grin. It was the truth. Edward had never learned to drive standard because the first car he drove had been an automatic that he shared with his mother. Every car after was also an automatic. But somehow, not having learned the art of driving a manual transmission made him feel slightly emasculated. "It's all right, I'll take the bus," he said while pushing himself up from the chair he had been attached to for over three hours in a row.

"Sorry, but you're not screwing with my transmission." Mike offered with empathy. "I'll buy some beer on the way home."

"It's all right. Really. I'll see you later," Edward entered the darkened stairwell and headed downward. He pushed the metal door open to the first floor and made his way through the parking garage looking for an exit to the street. It was almost completely vacant, except for the random scatter of cars still waiting for their drivers to claim them. *They sit in here five days a week,* Edward thought to himself. *I wish I had the keys to one of them...*

A loud slam echoed through the garage, interrupting his thoughts. He looked all around and stopped when he saw a female figure moving toward the driver's side door of a slick, silver BMW. He eyed the shapely woman as she got inside the car and started its engine. She took a moment to toss her pitch-black hair behind her before unfolding the visor to check the mirror. She pressed her lips together and flipped the visor back into place before shifting into reverse.

The woman then proceeded to drive backward violently. She backed past several parked cars and turned the corner before stopping hard. She then put it into first gear and drove as fast as she could. Her tires screamed, filling the entire garage with loud, horrible sounds before she had to slam her foot down on the brake pedal suddenly, stopping just before she would have hit Edward.

He watched her through the windshield. Her face was frozen and her eyes bulging. He thought that she was intensely beautiful. A part of him wished that she had hit him so that she would have been forced to help him up off the road. If he had lived through it, of course.

The woman opened her car door and stepped out in a light gray suit. Her jacket was fitted and the skirt hung modestly just below the knees. The sound of her black high-heeled shoes clicked on the pavement as she walked toward him.

"What are you doing? Are you all right?" she asked him. Her voice lacked the touch of concern he expected would have come from it considering the nature of the situation. "Do you work here?"

"I just started today," he told her boyishly.

"How did it go?" she asked sarcastically. Her face looked stern.

Edward couldn't figure out why he had just stood there when he saw her car coming. One minute he was watching her fix her sleek, shoulder-length hair, then the next minute he was watching her car advance toward him way too fast. He had been fantasizing about her and he wasn't about to admit it.

"I'm sorry," he told her.

She looked him over before speaking again. "What were you doing just standing there?"

"I didn't really have a chance to move," he answered. "You were going kinda fast."

"Was I?"

Edward had to think quickly. "I was on my way out. I'm taking the bus," he said before stopping himself. But it was too late to prevent the embarrassment.

She smiled and whisked the hair away from her face. "You don't have a car?"

"I do," he reacted quickly so she would know he was datable. "But it's in Austin. I just moved here and I haven't brought it up yet," he lied.

"Oh, so you have to take the bus. That's why you were standing around in the parking garage."

"Yes. No. You see, I was on my way out ... through there," he said as he pointed toward the daylight peeking through an opening to the street.

Edward's sense of desperation leaked into the logical part of his brain and was attempting to take it hostage. His body wanted her very badly even though he had only known of her existence for less than a few minutes. There had to be something he could do to get to know her better.

"Could you give me a ride home?" he asked. Completely out of character and lacking in tact, he had decided in an instant to lay it all out for her. This was his move. "I mean, we're coworkers, right?"

"Um," she frowned at him and then looked down at her designer shoes. He could see that she was trying to think of an excuse, any excuse, to get out of the uncomfortable spot he had just put them in.

"It's not really far from here," he tried again. "But I understand if you can't. You don't even know me. I could be a psycho," he laughed. He hated himself for giving her a way out. He was never going to have a chance to get close to a woman like her ever again and he didn't, and knew that he never would, have the balls to be as assertive as he wanted to be.

"No, I don't think you could be a psycho," she smiled. "Your hair is styled too neatly." She didn't think that a lanky man with mousy brown hair and a slouchy posture could do much harm to her. He gave off a happy-go-lucky kind of vibe— too simple to be threatening. Too naive. And in his shyness, he couldn't seem to keep his pale blue eyes on her for more than seconds at a time without a drop of sweat running down his stupid face.

"What?" he asked with what he thought was a witty type of smile. Conversation was an opportunity he hadn't expected, but he was more than willing to take the bait. "Lots of psycho-paths have had nice hair. It's only messy in the movies. What about Bundy?"

"Hmmmm," she contemplated. "Look, you seem like a nice guy, but this is my uncle's car and I'm only borrowing it. I don't want to risk getting it ... dirty. No offense."

"I'm dirty?" he asked with a playful grin before looking away. He realized now that he was flirting harder than he had expected to.

"No," she laughed deeply. Her mouth opened and he watched her enjoying his weak attempt at humor. Her teeth were perfect. "I have to return it to him soon and ..." she stopped and looked at him like he was a lost puppy. "Okay, get in."

He had done it. He was actually going to sit next to her. When he climbed in, he was extra careful not to touch any-thing. He folded his hands onto his lap and patiently waited for her to situate herself properly into the driver's seat.

She placed the car into first gear and turned toward him. "Where do you live?"

"I don't know," he half-joked. "Uh, it's on West something. By some park and a big spaghetti place in a red building ..."

"I know where that is," she said.

She drove fast. His leg muscles tensed as she took corners. It was obvious that she was in a hurry to get rid of him. Her face was preoccupied. He snuck a peak at her as often as he could. He was disappointed that she didn't seem interested. He glanced at her left hand to make sure that she wasn't wearing a ring. There was nothing there but a small, fresh cut.

"So," he started again. "This is your uncle's car?"

"Yes," she answered passively.

"So you would be taking the bus too if you weren't borrowing it, huh?" he tried his hand at humor again.

"No. I wrecked my car last week," she said without turning to look at him. "It's in the shop."

"That's awful. Were you hurt?"

"No."

He wanted her to slow down so he would have more time to charm her. There was only a slim chance that he might get her to realize how awesome he was. Random, desperate thoughts began to creep into his mind. Should he simply try to confuse her and take her down some side streets, hoping to get them lost together? Maybe he could double over and pass out. Mouth-to-mouth in a side alley could be kind of sexy.

"What's your name?" she asked him.

"Oh! It's Edward Bloodgood," he perked up. "What's yours?"

"Deidra."

"Wow, that's a pretty name," he said. "It suits you."

She smiled insincerely. "Everyone says that."

Just then a siren wailed from behind them. Instinctively, Edward glanced into the rear view mirror beside him to see which direction it was coming from. When he saw the police car's lights flashing at them, he turned to Deidra to see her reaction. She was looking closely into the rear view mirror above her head.

"Shit!" she exclaimed nervously. "I knew this would happen. I should have gone the long way."

She pulled the car over onto a side street, leading them into a darkened alleyway.

"What are you doing?" Edward asked.

"Pulling over."

"Here?" he pressed further, surprised that she didn't just pull over when they were still on the main road.

She turned toward him and leaned over to look him square in the face. "This is my uncle's car," she said with severity in her eyes.

Edward picked up a hint of her perfume and inhaled it, secretly enjoying it. "I know."

She twisted her mouth and looked at him with concern. "You don't understand. Dammit! I shouldn't have given you a fucking ride."

Edward was disappointed, but she was right. He didn't understand. He watched as she straightened her posture and positioned her stare straight ahead.

In the rear view mirror, Edward could see that there were two police officers sitting inside of the patrol car parked behind them. One of them stepped out and eased up to the driver's side window of the BMW as Deidra pressed a button to let it down. The officer bent himself at the knees and waist to look into the car. After glancing around at the car's interior, he focused his eyes on Deidra. His stare was longer than it should have been.

"You have a driver's license, Miss?" he asked, speaking to her profile.

"Yes," she replied without looking.

"Well, can I see it?" he pushed further.

She turned to face him and fixed her eyes on his badge. "Are you new?" she asked the officer angrily.

Edward looked at her with his eyes wide in disbelief. The officer stood erect and placed his hands on his hips before clearing his throat. "Step out of the vehicle, Miss," he instructed.

Deidra let out a big sigh and closed her eyes. Edward stared at her, waiting anxiously for her to open the car door and follow the instructions the officer had given her. She lifted her head into the air and her face relaxed. She smiled slightly and then opened her eyes. The Zen within her seemed to take control.

"Okay," she said calmly and then opened the door and stepped out into the heat of the Texas sun. "I'm in a big hurry. Could you just give me a ticket so I can be on my way?" she asked politely.

Edward could not see the officer's face as they spoke, but he could see by his body language that he was not going to let her get away that easily. At least that wasn't the plan.

The officer stepped over to the passenger side of the car and motioned for Edward to join them.

"Don't involve him in this," she requested. "My license is in my bag. I'm sorry I was speeding and it won't happen again. If you run me through your system, you will see that I have *never* had a ticket before."

As Edward stood, the officer turned to Deidra and let his mouth gape open. "Do you realize how fast you were driving? Never had a ticket before? I have never seen anyone take a corner the way you did back there. Do you even know how to signal?" he snapped at her.

"You're right," she agreed. "I just need to get somewhere. I wasn't thinking … and … I don't feel good, like I'm sick or something." She glanced at Edward quickly. It was like she was trying to tell him something with her mind.

The officer intercepted the peek at her passenger. He turned to him. "Who are you? Why didn't you tell her to slow down?"

"I …"

"Let's not involve him," Deidra said sternly.

The officer focused back on Deidra. He did his best to look intimidating, but Deidra only looked annoyed by it. He grabbed his belt and proceeded to rock back and forth from heel to toe. Edward thought that his reaction to her was quite appropriate. It seemed to be a very typical cop-looking thing to do.

"I think you had better watch how you talk to me," he warned while looking down at her, crossing his arms.

"I think *you* had better watch how you talk to *me*, rookie," she glared.

Edward panicked inside. Although he tried his hardest not to show it, he was using all of his strength to prevent himself from begging the officer to take him home so he could just forget about the whole stupid day he was having. He would have told him that he didn't really know the woman and that her attitude was not at all a reflection of how wonderful he thought all police officers were. It was an admirable profession. He would have told the officer about how he fell victim to the woman's vampy good looks and simply asked her for a ride. She did almost hit him with her car, but wouldn't he have done the same thing? She was gorgeous. Besides, who wants to take the bus? But before he had a chance to fully comprehend the situation or what to say, he heard the slam of a car door. It was the other policeman.

The second officer was older than the first by about ten years. He looked to be in his early forties. As he strolled up behind his younger partner, Deidra rolled her eyes and tilted at the hip.

"What seems to be the problem here, Missy?" the officer asked with a smirk on his face.

"This isn't very funny, Gene," Deidra replied. "Maybe you should keep your rookie on a leash."

The younger officer looked at his partner for permission to move in on her, but received only a pacifying smile. Deidra's brazen show of attitude toward the cops was proving to be quite a show.

"You can sit in the car now," Officer Gene told his trainee.

"What? She's been harassing me!"

"I'm about to harass you! Wait for me in the car. I'll only be a few minutes," the second officer said with authority before turning to face Deidra. He moved in closer to her. She stepped backward, leaning slightly with a look of disgust on her face. The officer was amused. Her reaction to him made him smile wide. "You on your way somewhere?"

Deidra glanced over at Edward and then back at Gene. "You know I am, Gene," she responded with hesitation.

"Frankie got you runnin' some errands for him? What's it this time? Secret DNA lab business or are you just doing a cupcake run for the little bossy fuckers?" Gene snorted instead of laughing. It was what he was known to do. His movements and speech were too rapid. He was on some kind of high, almost daily, but it was too hard to tell if it was from caffeine or cocaine. "You know how much they love vanilla cupcakes ... all that sugar gets them all twitchy."

"Yes. That's what's up. I'm doing a top secret cupcake run," she responded dryly.

"You think you're better than me. Don't you, honey?" He leaned in close, trying to intimidate her. "Who's your boyfriend?" he asked while nodding in Edward's direction. "Never seen him before ..."

"That's because he is a *coworker* and I am trying to take him home!" she interrupted quickly. Her voice was stern and domineering.

"Well," the officer began. "You sure took him the wrong way, didn't you?" Gene spoke with his teeth flashing bright. "Especially today."

The officer pulled out a gun from his holster and held it loosely in his hand. Edward flinched and then froze mentally, his eyes fixed on the gun.

"What are you doing, Gene?" Deidra asked as the officer reached into his pocket and pulled out a black object and began attaching it to the tip of the gun's barrel. "A silencer? You guys are issued silencers?" she gasped.

"Of course not, girly. I bring my own with me. Just in case I find myself in a rare situation like this one." He eyed her as he aimed the gun at one of the BMW's back tires. "You are in my jurisdiction, aren't you?"

"Gene! This isn't my ..."

He pulled the trigger and the tire went flat. The car leaned a bit in the back, crippled. Deidra closed her eyes and kicked the ground furiously.

"Why did you do that?" she yelled.

"Because I can. You think you have all the power, don't you?"

"This guy isn't even involved!" she yelled, motioning to Edward with flailing arms. "Why can't you control your fucking ego? Dammit, Gene!"

"You got a spare in that German piece of shit?" the officer teased.

"I don't know. You better hope so you stupid ass ..."

The second back tire was suddenly lost as Gene blew it out with a second shot.

Edward jumped back in fear. This man was entertaining himself. It was obvious that he was out to prove something. Deidra wasn't afraid of him, but that did nothing to ease Edward's concern for his own safety. These people were crazy and Edward was fighting the instinct to run.

Deidra looked at Edward and smiled nervously. "Get in the car."

"But ..." was all that Edward could think of to say. He still had a chance to run.

"He's not going to hurt you. Just sit in there and you'll be fine," she said to him like a mother would to a frightened child.

Edward got back into the passenger seat. He stared at the reflection in the driver's side mirror. Deidra was moving in closer toward the police officer who was busy now disassembling his gun.

"Thanks a lot, Gene," she spoke with colorful sarcasm. "You're never going to get anywhere doing shit like this. I hope you fucking choke on a doughnut."

The officer placed his weapon back into its holster, still wearing a large grin on his face. "Ya'll have a nice day." He stepped backward with a 1970s sort of strut until he reached the driver's side of his patrol car. Then he scanned her body like a pervert.

Deidra stood there and watched the patrol car pull away. Gene gave her the finger and she could see him laughing hysterically as he peeled off. She waited until he was out of sight before running around to Edward's side of the car and flinging the door open.

"Come on," she urged him. "We have to go."

"Why? What's going on?"

"God damn him! That gun wasn't even a regular issue ... I have to get to a phone ..."

"I have a cell phone," he offered.

"So do I, but we can't use it," she demanded.

"Why not?" he asked innocently.

Deidra pulled him out of the car by the arm and watched as he positioned himself in front of her. She tried thinking of the right words to say. Something that wasn't cliché. Something that wasn't too dramatic or movie-ish. She looked him in the eyes and grabbed his hands, placing them gently into hers. She held them and frowned at him, trying hard to show a nurturing kind of emotion. She wanted to explain to him that his life was now in serious danger. She wondered if she should shoot him and place his body in a dumpster or in the trunk of the stolen BMW, just to get it over with. She didn't think he had much of a chance any longer. But while contemplating what to do with him, she realized that she was thirsty.

"Do you want to get some coffee?"

3

"Where are you?" said the man's voice on the phone.

"I'm down the street from the car," Deidra replied into the receiver, faking calm as best as she could. "In some coffee house. The car is parked in an alley."

"I'll send someone for you. What did you say happened to the Beamer again?" the man's voice was agitated.

"He shot out the tires. I think he was trying to make me late or piss me off ... he was high or something. It was hard to tell what he was trying to do."

"He's going to get us into trouble," the voice replied.

"He's an idiot," she agreed. "He wants more jobs, but you see how he acts? His head is all messed up."

"I'll have my guys pick up the car. You stay there and I'll send someone to get you in less than 15 minutes."

"Look," she began. "Here's the thing ... I'm not alone. There's a guy here with me. He saw everything."

Silence.

"Um, hello?" she tried not to let her voice crack.

"How well do you know this 'guy'?" the man asked.

"Well," she looked over from the courtesy phone to see Edward sipping on a cup of decaf. Some instinct suddenly kicked in. She wanted to protect him. "Pretty well. We went to high school together ... old friend. It was his first day at work. He didn't have a ride home."

The man on the other end of the phone was in deep thought. He cleared his throat before speaking again. "I hate allergies. Are you having problems with them today?"

"Who isn't?" she laughed nervously.

"What's his name?"

"It's Bloodgood, I think," she answered nervously. "He is just ... a guy. Clean."

"Okay," the man hesitated for a few seconds. "Was anyone else around?"

"Yeah. I think the dumbass was training a rookie. I memorized his badge number."

"Good girl," he praised with excitement. "Bring your friend tonight. We'll have to make sure he doesn't talk to anyone about this."

"He's clean," she reminded him.

"I heard you."

The man hung up and she heaved a sigh of relief while placing the receiver down. She didn't know why she wanted to keep Edward from harm. None of what happened was her fault. She hoped that they would just dope him up and throw him in a field someplace for what he saw. But the truth was that he had a higher chance of being killed instead. She thanked the barista behind the fake marble counter and walked over to the red sofa Edward was sitting on and sat down next to him. She had at least done her part to give Edward a fighting chance and that made her feel good.

"So? Good coffee?" she asked.

"Yes," he replied, wondering what her phone call was about.

"What's the point of decaf?"

"There isn't one," he replied. He placed the large coffee mug onto the small table beside him and gave her his full attention. "You looked pretty serious over there. Is your uncle upset about the car?" he asked her.

"What? Oh ... no, he's fine," she answered. "But, um, there is something I have to explain to you."

"You wish you had hit me with your car earlier, huh?" he laughed. "I ask you for a ride and this is what happens. I mean,

I feel bad that I am in your way now. That cop was ... wow. He had some mental issues ... I mean, it's weird to shoot at peoples tires, but if that's the kind of game you guys play around here, who am I to say ...?"

Deidra scanned the area around them and then leaned in closer toward Edward's ear. "There are some people coming to pick us up, but I can't take you home right away," she said in a soft voice. The vibrations of her words tickled his ear as she spoke.

"That's fine," he said while trying to mask his overwhelming excitement. Even though he was slightly afraid of her, he couldn't believe that he was actually sitting next to her having a cup of coffee. But he didn't want to come off as a helpless burden either. "I understand. I can call my roommate for a ride ... he should be out of work soon. What about the car?"

"Don't worry about the car," she smiled. "I have to talk to you before we go."

"Okay," he said, bracing himself. The look on her face concerned him. He could see through her smile. "I can still call my friend if that helps."

"Do you know what a secret society is?" she asked quietly.

"I guess. Like the one at Yale? The bones with skulls and stuff?"

"Um ...Yes. Like the one at Yale, and Harvard, and all the others," she confirmed. "Sometimes there are other kinds of secret societies, ones that aren't connected with schools. Some are linked to politicians and other people in high places. You know ... big boys."

"Like the government," Edward added to make it sound like he knew what she was talking about.

"Right," she said, not so sure that he understood what she was getting at. He was an innocent. She felt some nagging obligation to help him survive whatever they were about to do to him, but knew it was probably hopeless. "Well, never mind." She stopped to think for a moment.

"Why?" Edward asked with anticipation. "Look, I read stuff on the Internet. I saw some videos before about this. I know about things," he said in a creepy tone.

Deidra smiled and giggled. "Yeah, I'm not so sure. Real secrets aren't on the Internet."

"Ok, I guess that makes sense. So who are you talking about?" Edward chuckled. "What are they doing that is so secret?"

"Nothing," she said. She smiled at him. She had done her part for him. "It's no big deal."

Edward straightened himself in his seat and picked up his coffee mug. "Oh. Is your uncle in a secret society?" He took a drink and watched her while she began to twirl a lock of her hair between her fingers. Her face looked serious.

"What?" she looked away from him and creases formed on her forehead as she rolled her eyes. "I shouldn't have offered you a ride home."

"What do you mean? I practically made you give me a ride. Is this about your uncle's car?" His voice was filled with concern and he turned his body in her direction, hoping that she would see that he was being sincere. "Is he being followed by a secret society?"

"No, forget my uncle," she looked at him and hoped that he would catch on soon. "Tonight is a very important night for Dallas. There is a big meeting that I am running late for because of that stupid cop."

"Someone is coming for you, right?"

"Edward, someone is coming for *us*. You have to go with me to this meeting," Deidra replied.

"That's okay. I don't mind waiting for you. Is it for your job?"

Deidra scooted closer to him. Her leg was touching his and she could feel him tense up. "No, it's not for my job. It's for one of those societies."

"You belong to a secret society?" he gasped, being careful to use a low voice. "I thought that only men could join those."

"I should have shot out *his* tires," she thought aloud.

"What do you mean?"

Deidra suddenly perked up and turned in her seat to face the glass panels that made up the front wall of the coffee house. A black sedan pulled up to the curb and waited.

"That's them!" she said as she grabbed her handbag and pulled Edward's coffee mug from his hand. "Now listen. Do not question anything. In fact, it would be best to just keep quiet."

Edward nodded blankly, not understanding how his day had become this surreal. He tried to pinpoint the moment in his head, that moment that marked the beginning of his decent into weirdness. But his thoughts became sidetracked as he focused on her face. He had become a schoolboy and his hormones had taken over.

He knew this was going to be bad. He should have run. In fact, he knew that he shouldn't have followed her to the coffee house and instead should have insisted on looking for the next bus stop he could find. The only rational part of his brain that was still functioning was beginning to think that when he first saw her, he should have ...

"Oh! And don't be afraid," she added coolly. "Just go along with everything I say. Okay, Eddie?"

"Okay." Being called Eddie was bliss when she said it.

She slammed his coffee mug onto the table next to them and headed toward the glass door. She glanced behind her to see if Edward was following, but she didn't need to. He was at her heels like a pet dog.

When she pushed the door open, her hair rushed in a wave behind her, whipping him in the face. She arched her back and held her head high. Her heels tapped against the pavement in perfect rhythm. She opened the back door to the black car and moved aside, motioning for Edward to enter first.

Edward hesitated only momentarily before getting inside. The windows were tinted black and he couldn't see inside at first. But when he did enter and saw the interior, he stepped inside with care. It was definitely a custom job. Red velvet seats against some type of thick, red velvet flooring.

Deidra got in and situated herself, leaning back into the seat. Her face remained austere. As soon as she slammed the door shut, they were off. The car went past the alley where they had their encounter earlier with Gene, and Edward noticed that the BMW was nowhere in sight.

They continued through the city until they reached the highway. They took an exit past city limits. The access road they traveled led them on a long, scenic route. Nothing but trees and barbed wire fences were sprawled out on either side of them. Edward assumed that the fences were meant to keep in livestock, but there were no animals to be seen.

They would pass an occasional house that looked to be on the verge of falling apart. It was hard to tell if the homes had been abandoned or if families actually lived in them. Edward glanced over at Deidra from time to time, waiting for her to give any indication that it would be all right to speak. She was daydreaming into the barren fields, never once turning in his direction.

The night sky consumed the day and they had still not reached their destination. Edward figured out that the meeting was going to be located far from the prying eyes of the general public and someplace isolated. Every big city in Texas was surrounded by miles of country fields. Many of the paved roads could turn from paved to gravel without warning. Their car made a turn onto one of those gravel roads and Edward forced himself to keep his mind alert. This was now the unknown.

When the car stopped, Deidra straightened up and clutched her handbag tightly. Edward watched her, hoping to piece together what to do next. A moment later, she touched his arm. She was looking out the window on her side.

"Do you see that building?" she asked him with a calm spark in her voice.

Edward leaned in closer toward her window to get a better view. "Yes."

"That's where we're going."

"Oh," was all he could say. The building looked run down. It resembled a barn that at one time could have been a functioning dance hall. He turned in his seat to glance out of the back window, looking for the lights of a town and saw nothing. "What is this place?"

"It used to be a bingo joint or something," she replied.

"It's in the middle of nowhere."

"That's why we come here." She opened the car door and stepped to the ground below. Her footsteps sounded crunchy against the mix of small rocks, broken pieces of glass, and grains of dirt they were using as a parking lot. She flicked her wrist towards her body, motioning for Edward to follow.

The driver of the black sedan remained inside and the two of them walked up to the lifeless building. Edward could make out the hum of murmuring voices coming from inside. He stopped suddenly in his tracks, creating scraping sounds beneath his shoes.

"It's a satanic cult, isn't it?" he asked firmly. Feeling proud of himself for figuring something out on his own.

Deidra turned to face him and placed a hand on her hip. "Yes, Eddie. You are tonight's sacrifice," she scoffed before continuing toward the old building.

Edward quickened his pace to catch up with her.

"Don't ask any more questions," she warned as they approached a large wooden door. Deidra banged on the doorframe and waited. The faint sounds of Vivaldi's "Allegro" moved through the air. Edward looked into the field surrounding them and noticed a scattering of cars hidden in the night.

The door swung open and a large man in a dark suit stood before them. His eyes were fixated on the trembling stranger standing next to Deidra.

"He's … a guest," she told the man guarding the entrance.

The behemoth frowned and moved aside and they proceeded to make their way into the meeting room. What Edward had expected to see inside was nothing compared to what he actually saw.

The interior was one large room that had been painted black. The floor was covered with smooth concrete that reflected the neon lights decorating the walls. A large bar occupied most of one side of the room. Bartenders in starched white shirts and black ties were busy mixing drinks and operating stainless steel blenders.

The darkness of the room did nothing to hide the odd appearance of the people mingling with one another within it. Edward's attempt to be coy about his blatant stares was met with failure. Each person he looked at was more unusual than the last. He did a double take when he saw a man that was dressed just like James Dean walk past. He was the spitting image of him, frozen in time.

They made their way to the bar and Deidra ordered two martinis while removing her suit jacket. "You should down this as fast as you can," she advised and slid the martini to him across the smooth granite bar top.

Edward sat on the bar stool next to her and drank the vodka martini in two painful gulps. A man in a black tuxedo walked up behind them and tapped Deidra on the shoulder. She flinched and spilled some of her martini on the silky long-sleeved blouse she was wearing.

"Hello, darling," the man said with an amazing accent.

She turned in her seat to greet him. Edward did a half turn to acknowledge the man and inhaled some saliva the wrong way, coughing a few times. The man in the tuxedo was holding a chain leash attached to a black, studded leather collar. The collar was being worn by a shirtless man standing next to the one in the tux. The shirtless man wore hot-pink vinyl pants and had the word "Bitch" tattooed in large letters across his athletic chest. He looked to be in his fifties and was missing most of his hair.

"Walking somebody else's dog?" Deidra asked.

"Yes," the man in the tux responded. He held an aloof demeanor. His accent was upper-crust. It was exactly what Edward imagined wealth would sound like outside of Texas. "His owner is in the bathroom and he asked me to watch him. It's aggravating, really. The man has been in there forever."

"What's up?" the man on the leash asked casually.

Deidra glanced at Edward and could see the shock in his expression. "I think we should talk about things without distractions," she suggested to the man holding the leash. His hair was perfect. It was dark with just the right touches of gray mixed in and styled into a side-part. His entire look reminded Edward of Cary Grant.

"He's no bother," the man replied. "Sit!"

The balding man immediately sat on the floor.

"Stay!" the man in the tux let go of the leash and stood between Edward and Deidra. He placed an arm around each one of their shoulders and smiled. He smelled like good bourbon and money. "So this is our new member!"

Deidra bit her lower lip as she smiled back. "If you want him to be, I guess. Unfortunately he already met Gene today." She responded.

"Yes, don't get me wrong, most police officers are of exemplary character ... well, some are ... but this one ... let's just say that he won't be making any future mistakes," The man said to the both of them. "My name is Franklin. Deidra sometimes calls me Frankie, but she is one of the few that can get away with it."

When she laughed, Edward relaxed slightly. "I'm Edward," he said.

"People call you Eddie, don't they?" Franklin asked.

He looked fit and attractive. Edward guessed that he was in his late fifties or early sixties. "Some do."

"Eddie, you have had the privilege of being friends with Deidra for how many years now?" Franklin asked warmly.

"Since high school. Right, Eddie?" Deidra interjected quickly.

"Yes," Edward agreed. "But I can't remember exactly how many years that's been ..." he replied, not even sure that she was close to his age or where she was from. She didn't look like she was in her mid-thirties like he was. She seemed younger.

"What high school did you and Ms. Bonaparte attend?" Franklin asked while placing his grip tightly around the back of Deidra's neck.

"It's kind of embarrassing," Edward answered, seeing the palms of Deidra's hands go flat against the bar top. "I was home schooled, but we lived in the same neighborhood for a while, so we hung out."

Franklin released Deidra and spun around as the balding man on the leash ran across the room and into a crowd of people, barking loudly.

"Somebody catch that bitch!" Franklin yelled before turning back to Edward and patting him on the back. "I don't mean to be a bad host, but we have a lot of things to attend to tonight. Here," Franklin pulled a gun from his coat pocket and placed it into Edward's hands before disappearing back into the darkness of the room.

"What's this for?" Edward asked Deidra, hardly able to get the words out of his mouth.

She nodded to the bartender for another round and popped an olive into her mouth. "They're going to make you kill Gene," she said without emotion.

4

Perhaps he couldn't really blame it on getting in touch with Mike again. Edward found Mike a month back while searching the Internet. He typed in Mike's name, the name of the university they once attended, and the graduation year. He clicked on the profile picture to make sure it was the right Mike and found out that he had landed a job with a company in Dallas, Texas. Edward had had so much trouble getting a job interview after graduation that he took a job at a video rental store. Before he knew it, he had become content moving up the ladder and into management. He thought he enjoyed it, but longed for regular office hours. Mike looked like he had really found a great place to work. He worked during the day, drove a nice car, and got to wear awesome suits.

They both graduated from The University of Texas. They weren't the type of guys to join a fraternity and the interest they both desired from girls eluded them. They became study partners. They spent numerous hours in the library together, cramming for tests and discussing the plots and makeup from their favorite B-movies.

They were both business majors. Mike's intention was to someday make a big impression in the corporate world. Mike had dreams of running his own company while Edward would be just as happy with an hourly wage, as long as it was stable.

Edward contacted Mike via email. He wrote him a quick message congratulating him on his success because he knew to open with a compliment, then added something about his own inability to find the perfect job for the perfect pay in Austin.

He told him that he had been working as the manager of a video rental store, but desired something more. When Mike emailed back, he told him that he would look into a job for him at the same company he was working for. Edward was more than surprised when Mike was able to get him an interview. He had discovered in recent years that people rarely did what they said they would, but Mike surprised him.

Still, if he could go back in time, he would have asked one of his friends in Austin to teach him to drive a standard before moving to Dallas. Maybe then he would be sitting in Mike's apartment that evening—slinging down a cold one instead of being forced to attend some high-dollar psycho convention.

"There's Franklin over there with Gene," she pointed out. "He's probably going to tell him something to get him to think that he's being honored tonight. That way, you will have a clear shot at him when he's standing next to that podium up there. After you shoot him, you'll be officially 'in'." Deidra finished her second martini and flipped the hair out of her face. "Then we can break for the drag race."

Edward felt ill. Waves of lunacy rippled through him as he turned to look at her. He searched her face desperately for a release from the nightmare he felt trapped inside of. He was drowning in visions of murder and middle-aged men dressed up in freakish, high-quality Halloween costumes. She didn't smile. She didn't mouth the words, 'just kidding' like he had hoped. All he had left to wish for was that a camera crew might pop out from the shadows and explain to him that it had all been a cruel prank set up by a network marketing team for the sake of TV ratings.

"Drag race?" he asked with a hardened face.

"Yep." She raised her hand and a cocktail waitress presented her with a tray of shots. "I'm racing Johnny Feinstein tonight."

Edward watched as she downed a shot and proceeded to grab another from the tray. "You people drag race?"

"It's fun."

"I can't wait to see that," he laughed.

"As soon as you kill Gene we can get to it."

"Fuck," he sighed.

Moments later a spotlight appeared on the floor before them. There was a cream-colored podium set up in the back of the room with a microphone attached to it. The spotlight found the podium and the microphone hit a high screech as it was turned on, drawing the attention of everyone in attendance. The crowd moved in and gathered themselves around, staring at the man who was walking up to begin the proceedings. It was Franklin. A small applause broke out and Franklin hushed the crowd by raising one hand into the air and bowing slightly, a sure gentlemanly gesture of modesty.

"Please," he spoke as the microphone cracked and popped in response. "I thank you all for your support. Now, let us get down to business."

The room looked like it held over 200 people. All of them now stood in silence. And at the same time, Edward was being dragged by the arm through their midst. Deidra was moving them in closer.

"Many thanks are in order tonight. This evening's catering is being provided by the R.G. Wheatherby Law Firm," Franklin paused long enough for a round of applause. "Also tonight I would like to report that our projected earnings from last quarter's events have far exceeded our most outrageous expectations! And you know they were outrageous!"

The room exploded into a roar of delighted applause and laughter.

"The deadline to place bets on tonight's race is fast approaching," Franklin motioned to an enormous clock above his head on the wall behind him. He had the voice of an animated game show host. Nothing like the more reserved and refined version of Franklin that Edward met earlier. "You have approximately ten minutes until 8 p.m."

Some heads within the assembly began to turn about, obviously looking for a way to finalize their bets before it was too late. Edward noticed a group of people with desperate-looking faces heading toward a small booth in one corner of the room.

"I want to keep this meeting short here tonight. We do have one more order of business to get to before we make our way to the track." Franklin reached behind him and picked up what looked like a bowling trophy from the floor and placed it on the podium in front of him. He had to lean over to one side to see past it and into the swarm of faces watching. "I would like to present this award to a longtime member for outstanding service to our organization. Gene Powell, get up here!"

The drunken police officer staggered through the mass of applause and then attempted to stand without swaying, next to Franklin, for a pat on the back.

"Before I present you with this award," Franklin said to Gene for everyone to hear, "I would like to introduce a new member. It's a funny story, but anyway ... Deidra, please bring up Edward!"

Deidra pushed Edward from behind and through the crowd as he tried to think of a way out of the building. Deidra must have removed the gun from her bag when he wasn't watching because he jumped when he felt its cold metal barrel being slipped into the back of his pants, leaving it concealed behind his suit jacket. It rubbed against his spine as he was walked. She gave him a final push from behind and then all the eyes of the room were on him.

Franklin greeted Edward with a pat on the back as he approached the podium and stood staring into the audience in front of them. Edward stood between Franklin and Gene as

Deidra looked on from the front row. He could feel Franklin's hand glide down his back and then halt suddenly when he felt the handle of the gun that had been placed there.

Franklin moved closer to the microphone and continued, "Please welcome Eddie into our circle of friends!"

Edward braved an uneasy smile and looked at Gene who was practically falling over and drooling on his cheap, shrunken suit.

"Edward is being brought into our little club because of Gene," Franklin stated with a twisted grin. "Isn't that right, Gene?"

Gene's reaction was more than delayed. He turned to the blur that he thought most resembled Franklin and forced his smile downward into a frown. It was the kind of exaggerated frown that a rodeo clown might paint on his face. He stumbled and tripped on himself, arms outstretched for the microphone like a clumsy toddler and pulled it to his drooping lips. "I dunno this guy," he slurred, pointing at Edward.

He let go of the mic and swung it back into its place as the audience laughed at his sloppy antics. Gene staggered back to his previous spot next to Edward, stomping his feet down and waving at a waitress for another drink.

Franklin moved away from the mic and whispered into Edward's ear, "Pull out the gun."

Edward looked at him in disbelief.

Franklin returned to the microphone. "Yes, he's very cute, isn't he?" Franklin's condescending tone quieted the room. "Officer Powell risked the exposure of our very profitable organization today. Once again, he decided to do something imbecile in public. He played a childish prank in front of another police officer and in front of this fine young man here."

Edward didn't move. The crowd's jubilation sank and was quickly replaced with tension. They knew what was coming. And yet Gene was oblivious that his fate had been determined that night. He swung his body around to face the podium, his mouth ajar.

Franklin placed his hand firmly on Edward's shoulder and squeezed, "I don't know how many times I have let Officer Powell get away with embarrassing the city of Dallas and the state of Texas, but it is time for that to end." Franklin reached behind Edward and pulled out the gun from beneath his jacket and aimed it coldly at Gene.

"Do you have any last words, Gene?" Franklin asked with his head tilted back arrogantly.

Gene shook his head. He did not have any last words. His eyes went blank as he urinated in his pants.

Franklin handed the gun to Edward, taking care to keep its aim steady upon Gene. "Shoot him, Eddie," Franklin commanded. The cruelty in his voice frightened Edward beyond words.

"I ... I can't," Edward stammered. He was close to soiling his own pants.

Franklin held his hand to his mouth to cover a giant smile and then burst into laughter, pointing a finger at Gene. "You should see your face!" he yelled. "The gun's loaded with blanks, Gene! You see how it feels now?"

The room's morbid silence gave way to laughter once again.

"Go ahead," Franklin said to a frozen Edward with a grand smile, "Shoot him so we can give him his fucking trophy," he managed between laughs.

Gene looked down at his damp crotch and burst into laughter himself. "You bastard!" he called out to Franklin.

"Go on," Franklin urged Edward. "Pull the trigger!"

"Yeah! Shoot me, you pussy!" Gene teased.

Edward relaxed his grip and the gun lowered slightly. He allowed his finger to pull the trigger and a bullet entered

Gene's right thigh. Gene screamed and fell to the floor. The room went silent.

"What the hell was that?" Franklin scolded, losing his gentlemanly composure. He snatched the weapon from Edward's claw-like grip. Edward's hand had tightened around the gun when he saw the blood begin to gush like a fountain from Gene's leg and realized that it had not been a joke. Franklin stepped over to Gene who was lying on his back, clutching his leg and wincing in agony on the floor. Franklin stood over him and shot him three times in the chest. Gene was dead.

Franklin dropped the gun down on top of Gene's body and stepped over to the podium's microphone. The sound system's feedback screeched throughout the room, causing many to flinch. "Who wants to see a race?" Franklin asked enthusiastically. The spark in his eyes was back.

The entire room roared and cheered vibrantly in return.

5

Somehow, Edward ended up back inside the black sedan. He didn't want to look, but he knew that Deidra was at his side. The car was heading down what appeared to be an abandoned road. He could feel Deidra's eyes on him often, but he ignored her. He couldn't remember getting back in the car. The velvety red interior made him want to throw up. It only served as a reminder of the blood he saw shooting out of Gene's chest moments earlier. He was sure that if he had been coherent enough at the time, he would have refused to get back in.

Deidra placed a soft hand on top of his. As Edward recoiled, she slid herself across the velvet seat and leaned against him.

"Hey," she said gently.

"Leave me alone," he responded, gazing out into the stars hovering outside. Their twinkling reminded him of a painting he once knew during an art history class. He took the class as a credit requirement and had no intention of being turned into some kind of an art geek. He couldn't even remember the name of the painting after graduation, but he liked it.

"I know you hate me," she said to him. "You didn't kill him though, Franklin did. It's a way to cement your connection to us, to prove your loyalty. We have to be able to trust you. So let's just hope he forgets about it and doesn't make you perform a do-over."

Edward turned to her and screamed at the top of his lungs, "What the fuck do you mean a do-over? They think they can get me to kill someone ELSE?"

Deidra backed away from him and watched as he spat his anger at her. "Get a hold of yourself, Eddie!"

"Don't fucking call me that! I don't know you! My name is Edward!" he screamed.

Deidra placed a gun to his temple and Edward slipped into darkness. He went numb and swallowed hard. There was pain in his throat at the thought of her blowing his brains all over the car and leaving him to die in some field. Texas is pretty big. He was sure that no one would ever find him or hear of him again.

"Edward, calm yourself down. I don't want to have to kill you," she begged.

Edward opened his eyes again. He was going to get through whatever the hell he was being put through. He would be strong. "I'm sorry," he said feebly.

Deidra pressed the tip of the gun hard against his head, "Don't ever yell at me again," and with that, she put the gun down and placed it under the car seat.

They continued on peacefully toward what he could only assume was the race all the freaks had been so excited about. She was right after all. Franklin had killed Gene. He shouldn't have taken it out on her, even if she had forced the gun down the back of his pants. They probably brainwashed her into doing it. *Damn, Edward. Quit making up excuses for her. She's still a psycho!*

They were only a small part of a long caravan of cars, trucks, motorcycles, and various forms of sport utility vehicles driving down the road. Every person at the meeting had loaded themselves into something expensive and, for the most part, black with tinted windows. To Edward, he was being escorted to his own funeral. *Funeral*, he thought to himself. He wondered now what they would do with Gene's body.

He could see up ahead on the road that their parade was turning into a wooded area. They drove through the trees with confidence like they had done so a hundred times before. After a few minutes, there appeared before them a clearing where people were parking. Beyond the parking area were some bleachers that looked like they belonged to a high school track.

As the sedan stopped, Deidra inhaled a deep breath and released it forcefully. She shook out her wrists and arms in front of her. She tilted her head from side to side, extending her neck, loosening up.

When the ritual was over, she opened the car door to make her way out toward the bleachers. Edward sat alone inside the car and watched her disappear into the bustle of people opening and slamming the doors of parked cars all around him. He laid his body out across the warm velvet seat to let his face sink into its ugly beauty. He thought about his mother describing a dress that she made out of red velvet for her prom. She was a free spirit that had convinced her date to wear a suit made entirely of the same wondrous material. He could smell exhaust in the air. It seeped into the car because that evil bitch Deidra hadn't even bothered to close the door when she left. Edward could see his mother crying with him when he fell down the stairs as a little boy and hit his head. The concussion came on strong. *The gun is under the seat.*

A shadow covered him and he turned his face upward to peer out through the open car door. Franklin's silhouette was in view.

"Eddie, this is not the time to take a nap," Franklin teased.

Edward was afraid of Franklin's mental state and did not want to trigger his bad side. He raised himself up and stood outside the car. Franklin smiled and looked him over.

"You're lucky I like Deidra as much as I do," Franklin began. "Because you were a witness to Gene's mistake … it could have been your death sentence."

Edward, having lost all hope for a normal evening, straightened his posture and made a pleasant facial expression that he might use in a normal social situation.

"Life will surely be different from what you were used to before. But, you should find that it can be nice to know people of influence. Of course, we will have to put you to work. You can't be a member without providing something in return." Franklin explained, tilting his head and glancing upward in thought. "What is your degree in, Eddie?"

Edward looked past Franklin and could see that groups of people were seating themselves into the bleachers across the field in front of them. "Marketing." The zombie part of him spoke. "I work at Corpotex."

"Marketing! Wonderful!" Franklin was overjoyed and clapped his hands together firmly. "Eddie, we can use your talents! Most definitely. But enough of that for now. There are more important things at hand, my friend." Franklin spun around on his heels like a teenager and Edward noticed that upon his shiny black Italian leather shoes were a pair of old fashioned white spats, reminiscent of the kind he had seen in a number of black and white gangster movies. The only thing missing was a Tommy gun. Franklin motioned for Edward to walk alongside him as he strolled toward the spectators preparing to see the race.

Edward couldn't believe his eyes as he got closer. As they approached the open area just before the stands, Edward spotted Deidra pacing before a pastel pink hearse, speckled with bits of silver glitter and adorned with a gleaming, porcelain-white hood scoop. Franklin smiled and asked into the air, "Aren't they beautiful?"

"What?" Edward asked, having to pry his eyes away from the enormous Cadillac to allow himself to gaze upon the other strange vehicle parked next to it. It was a glossy black ambulance complete with a skull and crossbones painted on each side.

Edward walked all the way around it and stopped to stare at the front where instead of the word 'ambulance' the words 'fuck you' had been painted backward in its place. Standing before the oddity was a small man dressed from head to toe in black leather, sporting a dark green pompadour hairdo and thick side burns to match. The man looked far from the cool image he was trying to project. His thick, black-rimmed glasses and buck teeth made him look like a skinny Elvis reject. The man kicked one of the ambulance's white-walled tires with his snake-skinned cowboy boots in an awkward display of masculinity.

"This is a race we hold once a month," Franklin explained. "It has become the highlight of my life."

Edward looked at Franklin to see that he had become misty eyed. He couldn't understand why a man who appeared so classy would be interested in a drag race. To make it even more perplexing to Edward, was the added fact that the vehicles being raced were not of any professional racing pedigree, but more along the lines of novelty in nature. Franklin seemed far too refined in character to be interested in something as trivial as drag racing. The bets placed on these races had to be what made something so off-key acceptable to these people. It must have been profit-motivated.

"These beauties are works of art in motion," Franklin professed deeply. "I'm sure you are wondering why we would risk damaging them like this in a silly race."

"I guess," Edward answered, not really sure what he was wondering at that moment. He had been too busy watching the tiny Elvis try to catch a glimpse of his own reflection in the glossy paint job of the ambulance.

"A part of the beauty of this race is the outcome. Life presents us with many things that are beautiful, but those things are rare and even the most beautiful thing will not last forever," Franklin spoke in a manner that was meant to sound philosophical and profound.

"Why are they ... *these* and not real race cars?" Edward asked. "I mean they can't be that fast."

"That's the part that makes it interesting. Personally, I don't care about 'real' race cars. We already know they're fast. But these cars present more of a challenge."

Edward found himself becoming lured in with interest while at the same time remembering that he was speaking to a man that murdered a police officer about half an hour earlier. "So you take bets and then race."

"Basically."

"Just two cars ... or whatever they are, at a time?" Edward asked.

"Each vehicle represents a successful business or a corporation. It changes all the time. In fact, I'm sure you already know that Deidra is racing tonight."

"Yes," Edward answered.

"She is one of our best racers. Corpotex has won many times with her."

"Oh," Edward responded.

A loud speaker crackled as an announcement blared from a small booth situated at the top of the bleachers. "Attention racing teams. Prepare for pre-staging. This is your 5-minute warning. Repeat. Prepare for pre-staging. This is your 5-minute warning."

"I must take my seat, Eddie," Franklin said.

"Where should I sit?" Edward asked.

Franklin chuckled lightly and then smiled at him. "I would really like for you to ride with Deidra tonight."

"But ... why?"

"For the whole experience. Art is meant to be an experience. You need this in order to understand."

Edward couldn't handle much more insanity. The idea of sitting inside an old pink hearse while it raced an ambulance driven by a green-haired Elvis should have been enough to push him over the edge. But to Franklin, it was another form of initiation because almost killing a guy had not been enough. "What if we crash?"

"You'll be fine," Franklin tried to assure him. "If I could bet, it would be on Deidra to win."

As Franklin made his way toward the stands, Edward stood alone, starring at Deidra. She was arguing with a man in a mechanic's jumpsuit while pulling her hair back into a messy ponytail behind her head. She kicked off her high-heeled shoes and traded them for a pair of motorcycle boots with large silver buckles and metal iron crosses on the sides. One of the men on her team scurried to take her heels from the ground and the handbag from her arm. Deidra spotted Edward watching her and rolled her eyes at him. He was about to put his life in her hands.

Edward walked over to her and lifted his brow. "I guess I'm riding with you," he said.

Deidra stepped away from the hearse and a man from her team got inside and started the engine. "Whatever," she said, watching closely as the hearse and the ambulance were driven to a spot on the lanes just in front of the bleachers. Franklin was seated in the front row, surrounded by a group of men dressed in suits. Edward swore that there were more people at the race than in attendance at the meeting earlier. He wondered how such a large group of people could keep this whole operation quiet. He thought back for a moment and wondered how the waitresses and bartenders at the old bingo hall were going to be kept silent. *Could it really be that secret?*

Edward shook himself to attention and noticed Deidra getting into the hearse. "Wait!" he called, running full speed. He ran until his hands slammed into the car with a thud, preventing the rest of his body from hitting it. He leaned his hands against the passenger side door and looked inside at her.

"Get in," she said with disappointment.

Edward got in and pulled the heavy door shut with both hands. The interior was black and he could smell a coconut fragrance inside. "It smells like a Pina Colada in here," he told her.

"Shut up."

"Please don't be mad at me, Deidra. Try to understand why I freaked out in the car earlier. I don't kill people. I rent movies and play video games sometimes. I've killed people in video games. That doesn't count."

Deidra placed her hands on the large steering wheel and gripped it tightly. Edward noticed that Franklin had made his way over to a part of the bleachers that were empty. He stood in front of them with his hand outstretched as if trying to complete an imaginary handshake. And for a moment, he could see Franklin smile as a shimmer of ghost-like bodies seemed to appear from nowhere, sitting in the empty seats, and then disappear. But he didn't have time to think about it. His life was in danger.

He looked around the cab for a stick shift. "This thing is an automatic?" he gasped with surprise.

"Of course it is," she shot back at him.

"How the hell is this thing supposed to win against an ambulance anyway? An ambulance is meant to go fast and a hearse ... isn't!" Panic took a hold of him.

"All I know is that this thing has a V8, 500 cubic engine. Other than that, it looks hot and it's loud. I don't care about much else," she boasted.

Edward looked over at the ambulance parked next to them and could see the driver standing in front of it putting on a pair of black leather racing gloves. "I still think ambulances are faster," Edward protested. "And didn't I see you drink a tray of shots back at the ..."

"Shut up!" she yelled for silence. "Do you want me to win or kill us both in a fiery crash? I need to concentrate. Speed is not always as important as concentration. It's all about reaction time."

Edward looked dead ahead. There would be no more interruptions from him. He wanted to live through whatever was about to happen.

The loudspeaker crackled to life again and the sound of a drum roll floated through the air. The audience shifted their focus from personal conversations to the cars parked before them on the ground. Many of the patrons opened up their cell phones or computers as the announcer began, "Welcome, ladies and gentlemen. We are pleased to present to you tonight's race."

The stands were overcome with applause.

"Tonight we present our reigning champion against a competitor that has recently qualified to compete in their first race," Edward noticed that the announcer was careful not to mention any names. "Our challenger will be driving the black, 1993, Type III Ford ambulance. It has been equipped with its original strobe emergency lights, siren, and PA."

The announcer stopped as Johnny let the siren wail and the lights flash to the accompaniment of thunderous applause.

"The Type III ambulance is a mid-sized model with a box welded to a van chassis. Its smooth-shifting transmission and V8 diesel engine make it a must in a life or death situation. Let's hope we won't be needing it for after the race, folks!"

The crowd celebrated with more applause before the announcer moved on to describe the next grim machine.

"Our champion will be driving the pink 1973 Cadillac hearse. It has been classified as one of the longest hearses in funeral history. It has also been referred to as a 'combo hearse.' Its backside panels can be removed and a siren attached to the hood for quick conversion from hearse to ambulance. Either way, it's a scarrrrry ride!"

The audience roared with laughter.

"Underneath its soft but gruesome shell is a raging V8 engine." The announcer paused as Deidra revved the engine loud enough to cause an outbreak of excitement to emanate through the stands.

The drum roll ended.

"Our starter may approach the lanes," the announcer stated.

Edward hit his head on the plastic slide window behind him separating the hearse's front cab from the back as the starter appeared from the stands. It was someone dressed in a full-bodied alien costume. Its large pale head and black almond-shaped eyes startled him. It looked too realistic. *It has to be a costume.*

The alien waved its elongated fingers toward itself and then stopped after Deidra and Johnny pulled their vehicles inches forward to the thick white line drawn before them.

"Our racers are now staged," the announcer informed the audience.

To Edward, it was as if all sound ceased to be. The starter raised one creepy arm into the air, and then let it down as Deidra and Johnny forced their awkward vehicles down the lanes. Edward screamed as the ambulance and the hearse whizzed past the alien. He was sure that one of them would clip its body.

Edward watched as Deidra leaned forward, giving the accelerator all of her might. She was ahead of the ambulance and before he could remember to cover his eyes, they were across the finish line.

Deidra rejoiced loudly. "Yes!"

"That wasn't so bad," Edward said with his teeth clenched together. To his relief, Deidra was pressing on the brake. They were slowing down smoothly. And more importantly, they were alive.

"It's only an eighth of a mile long," she mentioned casually. "It's almost nothing. Seconds. It's all about reaction time."

She turned the hearse around slowly and proceeded to drive in the grass toward her team of mechanics in the make-shift pit area. Edward's heartbeat was returning to normal ... whatever that was at this point.

The ambulance pulled up alongside them as they parked. Edward sat for a moment and closed his eyes. He could hear voices over a microphone in the background and then Franklin's voice echoing between the sound of hands clapping.

Deidra got out of the car. He opened his eyes out of curiosity and looked toward the sounds of activity in the stands. He could see some type of ceremony going on. Franklin was holding a microphone and standing next to a man he recognized as his new boss at Corpotex, Mr. Bennett, and another man. The other man was being handed something. It was brown.

"What is that?" he asked Deidra through the open window as she stood outside to watch the proceedings.

"It's a ceremony," she replied.

"No, I mean that thing that man is being given?"

"It's an envelope," she answered.

"Who's that guy Franklin's giving it to?" he asked.

"Mr. Davis, fuckhead!" Johnny Feinstein yelled into the passenger side window before pulling the door open violently. He grabbed Edward by the jacket and threw his body to the ground. "He's my boss!"

Deidra ran around to the other side of the hearse to stop Johnny, but he was already on top of Edward, punching him repeatedly in the face. "Stop!" she screamed.

Members of each racing team ran over to witness the assault on Edward's face. They watched for a few seconds before Deidra convinced them with her screams to help break it up.

Johnny kicked and flailed as he was separated from Edward and pinned to the ground by two large men from Deidra's team. The two men argued in Spanish about what to do with the green-haired punk until Johnny finally gave up and relaxed his limbs.

"Pinche bitch!" Deidra yelled as she kicked Johnny in the side. The two teams of mechanics laughed at Johnny mercilessly until tears came from his eyes. They were not tears of pain, but tears from losing what could have been the most important race of his life.

Deidra turned to Edward and helped him up off the ground. "I'm so sorry," she said while dusting him off. "Are you hurt? Your eye is bleeding."

"Yes, I'm in pain," he answered with a sting in his voice. "Can we go now?"

Franklin made his way over to the scuffle's aftermath wearing a smirk on his face. He strolled past the group of men standing over Johnny and then looked at Edward. All of them stood at attention as Franklin turned to look each and every one of them in the eye.

"I was trying to conduct a ceremony up there," he pointed to the stands in the distance behind them. "Are you all a bunch of animals?" he asked sternly.

Many of the men shook their heads to indicate that they were not.

Franklin walked over to Deidra and smiled. "Congratulations once again, my dear," He then turned to Edward's swollen face and grimaced. "My dear boy. I apologize for Mr. Feinstein's inappropriate behavior tonight."

"That's alright," Edward managed to say through the intense pain in his mouth.

"Deidra, let's get this young man some drinks and something to eat," Franklin insisted. He looked at Edward's face and shook his head in disapproval.

"No, that's okay," Edward objected. "I should really be getting home now ..."

"But, Eddie, we always have a nice, private dinner with the winner after the race. Mr. Bennett will be there. You should be proud! Corpotex won again!" Franklin reminded him. "Besides, we can't let you go yet. What if you have a concussion? We should keep an eye on you for the rest of the night."

"Oh ..." Edward replied with disappointment.

Franklin turned to the group of mechanics standing around Johnny and smiled. "Take Mr. Feinstein someplace desolate and beat his face in for me."

Johnny's eyes widened.

"Yes, sir," they replied in unison.

6

Mike sat, half-awake, with toast crumbs falling from his lips and onto the floor below. His coffee was instant and its texture felt thick against his tongue. He couldn't wait to get to work and order a tall cup of gourmet-blended brew.

He had waited up most of the night for Edward to get home. He called his cell phone several times but it would forward to voicemail. Mike passed the time drinking a few beers by himself and then watched an old movie starring Paul Newman and Elizabeth Taylor. It was a drama. He wouldn't have normally found that type of thing interesting, but the repeated use of the word 'mendacity' clung to him. Whenever he raised the remote control to change the channel, again the word 'mendacity' would prevent him from actually doing it.

Mike reached for his wristwatch and put it on. It was 6:28 a.m. He looked at the coffee table in front of him and stared at the keys lying on the glass top. He had to make up his mind. He had been struggling with the idea of what to do about Edward's absence since waking up. Should he call the police or just go to work and hope to see him there? Mike didn't see Edward as the type to stay out late. He also knew that he didn't possess the skills to stay at a girl's place on the first night.

Mike heard a sound at the front door. There was a thud followed by some movement of the doorknob. It jiggled slightly, then furiously. Mike jumped to his feet and looked through the tiny peephole in the door. Edward was finally back.

Mike opened the door to see Edward slumped over, leaning against the doorframe. "Edward! What happened to you?" he asked. Mike could see Edward's suit jacket lying on the stairs outside the apartment, flapping in the cool breeze that had been forecast for that morning.

Edward struggled physically to make his way into the apartment. His shirt was halfway untucked and his belt missing. He walked into the kitchen and opened the refrigerator to grab a beer. He picked out a bottle and twisted off the cap.

"Edward!" Mike called to him in shock. No man in his right mind would drink a beer in the morning. "What are you doing? We have to go to work! Where have you been?" Mike was out of breath.

Edward slammed the bottle down on the countertop and looked up at Mike who was still standing in the doorway with his arms raised upward, frozen like a mannequin on display at a department store. Except for the horrified expression on his face.

"I'm not going to work today. I had a bad night," Edward told him and then took another drink.

"Edward! Are you out of your mind? You just started yesterday! You can't skip out already!" Mike couldn't contain his anger. He was livid. It was his reputation on the line and it appeared that Edward couldn't have cared less. "What did you do last night?"

Edward smiled with his eyes wide. "I don't know." He looked like a man that had crossed that thin line between ordinary and the unnatural.

"Jesus!" Mike yelled and slammed the door shut behind him. "Get dressed for work, you're going in!"

"No fucking way!" Edward retaliated. "I don't feel good."

Mike forced himself to relax as his curiosity overwhelmed him. "You look like you've been blown up."

"I wish I had been," Edward replied.

"Dude, when you didn't come home last night I got kinda worried and started thinking that you got on the wrong bus that took you out of town or something. But then I started watching this show on TV about amnesia and..."

"Mike?" Edward asked. "When you get to work can you tell that guy with the red ... Jason ... that I have a fever and that I'll be at work tomorrow?" he pleaded with a tinge of whine in his voice.

"Damn, Edward," Mike said. "It's your second day." He didn't hide his disappointment.

Despite everything that he had been through in the last 13 hours of his life, Edward did not want to upset Mike. He chugged the remainder of his beer and opened up a box near the couch that simply had the word 'clothes' written on it. He pulled out a polo shirt and a pair of brown slacks. In front of Mike, he clumsily took off his torn pants and put on the clean pair. The fresh pair had creases in them from being transported from Austin, but Edward didn't notice. If he had, he wouldn't have cared. As he put on his new shirt, Mike shook his head in disapproval.

"What?" Edward asked.

"You have a black eye and there's blood on your face."

"This is how I'm going."

"You just drank a beer!"

"I'm READY TO GO," Edward confirmed.

They arrived at work on time. Mike parked his car, switched off the engine, and then looked back at Edward's slouched body. His legs were outstretched and occupied the entire back seat of his car. Edward picked his head up to watch as other employees left their cars to settle into their daily routines inside their snuggly cubicles. *Their world is made of right angles and bathroom breaks*, he thought.

"You smell," Mike said with an upturned nose.

Edward opened the car door and headed for the stairwell that would lead him to the third floor. Mike sighed and Edward knew that he already regretted letting him move in. He and Mike had been close in college, but people change. He stood outside of his car and called out to Edward, who was already opening the metal door to the stairs, "See you later, okay?"

As Edward stepped onto the third floor, coworkers stared. Jason dropped his jaw when he saw him and ran across the room to greet him. "Mr. Bloodgood!" Jason exclaimed.

Edward stopped and smiled weakly. He had been busy thinking about what color his vomit might be against the annoying green carpeting beneath his cheap department store shoes. "Hey."

"Mr. Bloodgood, please accept my apologies! I guess we made an error somewhere along the line ..."

"What are you talking about?" Edward asked. Jason's movements were too fast in comparison with Edward's nausea. He swallowed back a near mishap as Jason noticed and backed away.

"Your job requisite must have become mixed up with someone else's. I am so very sorry, sir." Jason ignored the stench of alcohol emanating from Edward's disheveled body.

"What's wrong? I didn't get the job?" Edward asked. He felt relief, thinking about moving back home and trying to forget that he had ever come to Dallas.

"No, sir. We placed you in the wrong department. Your office is upstairs," Jason said.

Edward's mind blanked out and he stared at Jason like he was waiting for the punch line of a joke. When it didn't come, Edward raised his eyebrows in exasperation. "How did I get an office upstairs?"

Jason frowned and then answered, "You work upstairs and everyone upstairs has an office. Would you like me to have your assistant take you there?" Jason asked with a tone that rocked between kindness and servitude.

"My ...?" Edward managed to stop speaking before possibly ruining a good thing. He composed himself and nodded his head to indicate that he did, in fact, want his assistant to show him to his office. He didn't think that he came off naturally when he nodded like a dummy, but he made the effort anyway, anxious to see his new office before they changed their minds and cancelled the employment offer entirely.

Jason told Edward to go on ahead to the fourth floor while he called his assistant to meet him in the lobby. The fourth floor turned out to be a paradise compared to the third. Real living plants hung from the ceiling and populated the walkway inside of ornate pottery. There was an indoor pond and it was active with fish and the sounds of a pump making bubbles. There was a calming scent that floated through the tranquil atmosphere, created in part by delicate track lighting.

Edward stood at the entrance as if he was in the presence of Saint Peter. *This is heaven.*

7

"Yes, she won it for us again," Franklin boasted proudly. He still loved actually talking on the phone. It, along with everything else he was interested in, seemed to be a dying art. "There's something about the way she competes. I can always count on her to try and show up the boys," he chuckled.

The phone had to be worthy of certain conversations in order for them to take place. Secured and scanned, the line was always still a risk. In some cases though, it showed the upper hand. It was a display of confidence that could downplay fear. A voice on the phone could only hide certain emotions.

"Oh yes," he assured. "I understand the implications. She won't lose. Things are set on our end."

Franklin studied his fingers as he listened carefully for specific vocal inflections. His smooth fingertips shined in the light of his office. Blank fingertips. Printless and untraceable. They had been taken from him years ago. He smiled when he heard what he wanted. "I am glad to hear how much they enjoyed it. It is always an honor to have them as our guests!"

He eyed a photograph of Deidra on his desk. Her eyes were heavily darkened with eyeliner and mascara the way he liked. Her lipstick was a perfect retro shade of red. "And they are welcome to her DNA at any time."

8

"Hello, sir," a man welcomed him at the entrance. "I am Anthony, your assistant."

"Hey," Edward responded, still a bit drunk from the vision that was the fourth floor.

"Allow me to show you to your office," Anthony suggested. He looked like he was in his 60s. His hair was almost all gray.

Edward walked with his eyes bouncing from room to room on either side of the hall. He was as distracted as a child at a theme park trying to take in everything at once. Anthony stopped at the end of a long hallway and opened the door to a room that was larger than Mike's entire apartment. "Wow."

"Yes. And my office is just across the hall from yours. My extension has already been programmed into your phone and is labeled. Please call me if you need anything, sir."

"Thanks," Edward replied as he gazed into the office. Normally, it would have been too ostentatious for his taste. But like many of those lottery winners he had read about in the news, once it was finally his, it became his new standard. There was a real oil painting on the wall and a large window behind the desk. The wood furniture placed throughout the room was a smooth cherry. "You don't have to call me 'sir.'"

"Would you like some coffee, Mr. Bloodgood?" Anthony offered.

"No, thanks. But," Edward was puzzled. "What should I do? You know, for work?"

Anthony pursed his lips together and looked to the ceiling. "I guess you should change your temporary passwords and log in to the network for today." He turned and walked into his own office across the hall.

Edward couldn't understand what had happened to the world that would require it to need the throngs of passwords, secret questions, and login IDs that seemed to be required of him and everyone else in corporate America. He was beginning to feel that the whole concept of computer security had been made up to give nerds more responsibility. They were the ones that programmed and let loose the viruses in college and now they were the ones being paid to protect the networks from the next generation of geeks. Perhaps it was all an elaborate nerd conspiracy organized to keep computer degrees valuable on the market.

He walked into the center of his massive office and felt the soft crushing of Oriental rug pile beneath his shoes. He was tempted to sit in the big leather chair behind the mammoth desk, but decided against it. He didn't feel right. Like the lottery ticket was a fake.

"Hey," a voice called to him from the doorway. "You like it?"

"Deidra!" Edward was actually happy to see her.

"Your face looks horrible," she told him.

Edward touched his hands to the sides of his mouth and cringed. "It's not that bad. No one else seemed to notice."

Deidra walked over to the window and looked out across the city. "Nice."

"Where's your office?" he asked, not knowing what to talk about since the embarrassment of the night before.

"It's down the hall," she answered. "But mine has a view of the other side of the city. Yours has more trees."

"I didn't think you liked trees."

"Why not?" she asked.

"You almost knocked one over last night …"

"No," she interrupted with patience in her voice. "We'll talk later. On the outside."

Edward looked out into the clouds. He thought about how strange Deidra was and at that moment wanted to get to know her better, even if it meant existing inside of some sub-reality once a month. He could see himself rubbing elbows with more ... interesting people. It might be good for him to diversify.

"I can give you a ride home tonight," she offered. "My car's out of the shop."

Her lips are so red and shiny. "Okay."

"Maybe we can stop for a drink," she said with a smile.

They are more of a burgundy color. "That would be nice."

They both turned when they heard a set of knuckles rapping on the open door. Mike stood there with his eyes wide. "How the hell did you swing this?" he asked with joy. Or jealousy. It was hard to tell.

"I don't know. I must really be good at something," Edward joked. He would have laughed, but his stomach muscles wouldn't have forgiven him for it.

"I guess so," Mike replied. He took a moment to eye Deidra and then reapplied his focus on Edward. They both had been standing at the window when he walked in and looked like they had been having more than a casual conversation before he interrupted. Edward cleared his throat and Deidra backed away from Edward's view of the city. She walked past Mike and left.

"See you later," she said.

"Bye," Edward responded.

Mike made a face at Edward and waited until he was sure that Deidra was out of hearing range before mocking her voice, "see you later!"

"Mike!"

"Edward!" he mocked him in return. Mike moved in closer to Edward and grabbed his arm to pull him in. "How do you know her?" Mike asked with concern in his voice. Or just plain nosiness.

"Why?"

"Because, Edward! She's not the kind of girl you want to be messing around with. Or even just be friends with!" Mike pointed out in a hushed tone.

"Why not?" Edward asked.

"Dude," Mike began with a stern face. "There's a rumor that she's, you know, sleeping with Mr. Bennett."

Edward could understand why such a rumor would have been started. Deidra represented Mr. Bennett at the race. They had probably been seen together on multiple occasions, perhaps even outside of work, discussing things related to the secret organization they were both a part of. Mr. Bennett was not her type. She was single. Absolutely single.

Edward had to play it smooth. "Oh. Well, I'll keep that in mind."

"Are you two going out later?" Mike asked.

"Maybe."

"Edward," Mike began in the voice of a father lecturing his sex-crazed son. "That's not a good idea."

"I'll be careful," he smiled.

After a long day of checking his personal emails and locking himself out of his new computer, Edward met up with Deidra in the parking garage and she drove them to a local bar. It was a nice place where the drinks were more expensive than they should have been. Very few of the beers were domestic. There were four pool tables, all of them occupied by men in dress shirts with ties hanging loose around their necks. Discussions focused on either women or business accounts. To many of them, the two were interrelated anyway. The jukebox played an assortment of songs by Journey and Boston. Edward and Deidra sat in a booth at the back. A piece of glass with gold decorative etching separated them from the booth behind them.

"Comfy seats," Edward commented, bouncing up and down like a child. "Nice!"

"I like this place," she smiled. "Okay, stop bouncing."

"So? Can we talk here?" he asked.

"Maybe we should start after a few drinks." She suggested.

Their server brought them each a beer. She talked Edward into trying a German Hefeweizen. She squeezed a lemon in it for him since he thought it was served with one merely for decoration. Their first beers went down with a conversation about Edward's former life in Austin. Edward told her the story of how he reconnected with Mike and how kind he thought he was to give him a place to stay until he had a place of his own. But any questions he would ask her about her personal life would be redirected back at him. She was a closed book.

By the time the second set of beers arrived, Edward was intent on learning more about the race he was forced to be a part of the night before. He leaned across the table and asked her a burning question, "What was in the envelope?"

Deidra tightened her jaw. Edward swallowed hard with anticipation and waited for her to give him an answer. She ran her finger down the side of her beer mug, guiding a drip of condensation down with it. She looked at him with pale green eyes and her face softened. "Did you read the paper this morning?" she asked.

Edward was afraid she was leading him off course again. "No."

"It might have answered your question."

Edward glanced around at the sides of the bar, looking for any sign of a discarded newspaper. He immediately stood up and made his way to the bartender and asked if he happened to have one, but he didn't. Edward searched his pockets for change and stepped outside and saw one of those newspaper vending machines and fed it some quarters. He grabbed the paper and ran back inside. Deidra watched him scan its cover and then quickly turned to a page further inside. He held the paper wide open in front of his face for a few minutes, ignoring Deidra as she sipped her beer. Edward closed the paper, folded it and then looked at her for more guidance.

"What company did … the loser run?" he asked.

"He's in the electronics business. It's called Humphrey & Davis Technologies. Or H&D Technologies," she answered quietly.

Edward leaned back in his seat. His back fell against the dark leather back board of the booth with a soft thud. His face appeared to be hypnotized. His eyes were distant, looking through the table before him. His lower lip hung heavy as his brain calculated what happened.

Deidra saw herself in him, the person she used to be. He was naive and still thought that the world would have something great to offer him if he only worked hard enough. There was still a sense of trust in the way he presented his words and in the questions he asked. He divulged things about himself and expected others to reciprocate. He still had no idea that the world had already taken him for all he was worth.

"He killed her?" Edward asked, his mind shaken.

Deidra nodded once in agreement and saw Edward's heart drop. His features became twisted and he held his mouth with a hand that quaked without mercy. He was doing his best to keep from falling apart in front of her, but felt such shame for what had been done.

"They have a choice. Usually, they take the envelope," she explained. "Are you all right?"

"No," he said and took another drink. "I don't want to be a part of this."

"You're not."

Edward flashed her a look of repugnancy. "What are you talking about?" he asked, his voice more elevated than before.

"If you don't lower your voice, I'm leaving," she threatened.

Edward's brain was spinning. He had a very limited set of options before him. He could cooperate with her and get more answers or he could cause a scene in front of the entire bar and risk being killed by a group of psychotic drag-racing enthusiasts. His fear of the nameless secret organization was growing. These people had proven that they had no qualms when it came to murder. He didn't want to be one of them; neither victim nor participant.

"How am I not involved?" he asked while having to force a kinder voice.

"Your identity is hidden," she said, leaning forward. "You don't exist the way you used to."

"I don't understand. I mean, that shouldn't matter. It's still morally wrong to ..."

"Eddie," Deidra interrupted softly. "It's not your problem. These guys have a choice. The loser is presented with two options. Money or death. It's not your fault if they love money more than their own moral obligations to others," Deidra tried to make him understand.

"I don't get it."

"They either let go of their top guy, or choose a hit. Usually, the closest person in their personal life."

"Okay," Edward closed his eyes just long enough to think of a way to form his next sentence into a discernible question. "So, they can fire their top ... revenue generating person, a salesman, attorney, chef or whatever fits their business description, or kill the person listed inside the envelope?"

"Right," she answered.

Edward looked down at the paper in front of him. Its corner was becoming soaked with the wet mess accumulating on the table. Their coasters were already falling apart and had become useless under their large mugs. "Why did it have to be his wife?"

"Each of the two opponents selects who they would want the other opponent to take out in advance," she spoke while her eyes scanned the room. "There is a great deal of research done before they select a name. It goes inside the envelope and that's that. Our guys must have thought that if he read the name of his wife, Mr. Davis would choose to fire his top guy instead. I guess they were wrong. It had to be a hard decision," she said with guarded sympathy.

"This is all about money, isn't it?" he asked.

"Of course it is," she answered. "Everything in the world is."

Edward glanced over at the wet paper again. "They chose her so he would be pressured to let go of his best salesman, or his CEO, or ..."

"Yes. They were hoping that he would get rid of, in his case, his top account salesman. It's all business competition taken to a higher level. All of this stuff matters further up the corporate ladder than we can see. Someone is linked to someone else and so on. They don't choose the wives that often though," Deidra said. "It only works on people who have a conscience. They must have read the guy wrong. You know, misinterpreted how strong his relationship was with her. His choices will come back to haunt him in the future though."

"He chose a salesman over his wife," Edward stressed.

"His *best* salesman. He probably brings in millions for him."

Edward furrowed his brow and glared at her. "Does that make it right?"

"I'm not here to pass judgment," she answered casually. "All I do is race ... and rough people up sometimes for collections ... and steal cars when I need to."

Edward shifted his focus as the third round of beers was delivered to them. He drank and allowed his thoughts to become diluted to the sounds of the jukebox.

"How did you get involved with racing?" he had to change the subject or risk saying something that might get him into trouble. He didn't trust her anymore. His attraction to her was still strong, but drastically jaded. Attraction to her now was not something he wanted to feel. It was now like having a twitch that wouldn't go away no matter how much he wanted it to.

"I have four brothers."

"Hmm."

"Do you have any brothers or sisters?" she asked.

"No," he was through for the night. "I think I should be getting back to the apartment. I'm really tired."

"You need a shower, too," she added.

Edward smiled. Every part of him regretted meeting her for a moment, but when that moment passed, she was all that he wanted again. It made him feel crazy and he hated himself for it. *Can I shower at your place?*

She insisted on paying the tab, which she did with a corporate credit card, and then offered to drop him off at Mike's apartment. Deidra was careful to drive the speed limit, so as not to frighten Edward in his already fragile mental state. She knew that the things he had learned was a lot of information to take in.

After he disappeared into the upstairs apartment, she checked the locks on her car doors and noticed that Edward had left his newspaper on the passenger seat. She picked it up and focused in on a small article about a city policeman that passed away in his sleep. He had a previously undiagnosed heart condition. He was a single father and had only been with the Dallas police for a few months. Deidra threw the newspaper down and slammed her fist into the steering wheel. "No!" she whispered.

9

There was a table and four chairs set up in the dimly lit room for the private meeting, as instructed. Franklin had been contacted on short notice by the powers that be and was honored to oblige. Being the gracious host that he always was, Franklin made sure to have only the finest in beer, wine, and hard liquor available for his honored guests. A last minute meeting was always an important meeting.

Franklin had been sitting alone in the room for an hour, nervous. He had no idea what was about to take place. He tried his hardest not to over analyze. The meeting could have been called for any number of reasons. Infinite reasons. He jumped when he heard movement outside the door.

Franklin stood erect and waited for his guests to enter. The door opened to three men in suits. Franklin smiled and motioned for them to be seated, "Please, gentlemen, make yourselves at home."

The three men took their seats as Franklin headed toward the door that had been left ajar. "Would any of you gentlemen care for a drink?"

"Yes," one of them spoke and looked around at his colleagues for agreement in his decision.

The oldest man had white hair and looked at Franklin with a grin, "I'll take a scotch."

"Make that three," a man in a brimmed hat said after conferring with the youngest man at his side.

Franklin waved his hand through the crack in the door, whispered to a man that appeared behind it, and was quickly presented with a tray of drinks. They each sat in silence until

Franklin populated their small table with napkins and beverages. Franklin's choice had been a glass of his finest pinot grigio, which he sipped only once before getting down to business. "What brings you to Dallas, my friends?"

The man in the hat answered, "We have come for two reasons. The first reason is to thank you for your organization's services. Our investors have been quite happy with the results."

"Thank you," Franklin replied.

"The second reason is to ask you for a favor."

Franklin raised his glass and took a hearty sip. "What can I do for you?"

"Mr. Andrews, your organization seems to have, over the years, perfected the art of ... getting rid of people flawlessly."

Franklin smiled proudly, "Yes. It is an art form few can truly appreciate. It does help that we have the funds with which to pull it off."

"My colleagues and I are here tonight to propose to you a new twist on your monthly race."

"I'm intrigued," Franklin sat forward, eager to hear any proposal that was meant to bring more excitement into his life.

"We propose that once a year, your race be conducted for a wild card."

"What do you mean?"

The white-haired man set down his glass and spoke with a raspy voice. "We're talking about companies competing for something new inside the envelope. Nothing else. They have to take the envelope no matter what. No choices. Makes things more interesting."

Franklin sat back and let the idea swim around in his head. "We could make the betting higher!"

"No," the man in the hat insisted quickly.

"But what would the contents of the envelopes be?"

The white-haired man touched the arm of the man in the hat before speaking, signaling that it would be his question to answer.

"We would want you to start this year. Maybe even next month," the man in the hat said. "There will be one envelope. You will go about your race and proceed with the ceremony afterward. Privately though, you will inform the head of each team that the format has been changed. The loser will carry out the task and be made to understand that carelessness will not be tolerated. Once the task is complete, the heads of each company will be paid. Everyone wins."

Franklin took a longer drink of his wine and looked into the eyes of his guests. "What would the task be?"

The white-haired man took control again. "We will tell you immediately after the race. Then you will let the team that receives the envelope know in private. You should present a fake envelope anyway just to make things look normal. We don't want any extra attention drawn to the race, even if it is from within the circle. This special condition is to remain top secret. The team carrying out the assignment will only find out from you, Mr. Andrews. They will have no choice but to carry it out as instructed."

Franklin knew that whatever the reason for altering the rules of his race, it had to be serious. He was clearly not being offered a choice in the matter. The format of his pet race was going to be different. But at least it was only once a year.

"Next month," Franklin mulled it over. "It's short notice, but I think we can do it."

"We knew you could," the raspy voice confirmed with a grin.

"Our next challenger hasn't been determined yet, but I can usually guess by watching the stocks. Corpotex is already set to race again," Franklin told them.

"In that case, we already know," the man in the hat assured him. "And we already have the task in mind, regardless."

"Oh?" Franklin wasn't surprised, but pretended to be.

"How long do you give your contestants to perform their current jobs?"

"The killings? 48 hours. Unless they put in for an extension which has only happened once."

"We will expect this assignment to be carried out at a specific time and place," the eldest man stated adamantly.

"I'm sure that will be no problem," Franklin said in response.

"We will determine the details and it is to be carried out exactly as we explain. We should have the specifics of that information shortly," the elder man said before pausing to cough. "This one's going to be big, Mr. Andrews. You must be careful to follow the rules we have set in place for a situation of this magnitude or we will be forced to shut your games down."

Franklin nodded. He was aware of his role as a subordinate to these men and their ominous superiors—aliens and the men secretly running the government. Exactly how they functioned in their decision making and why, he did not know. All he knew was to follow the orders he was given with no questions asked if he wanted to profit from them. He had once been his own boss, but by accepting the government's financial assistance, it had become much more than a partnership. Then when the aliens got involved, it became a lot more serious. Both groups of investors knew that he would do nothing to jeopardize his race. They left its operations under his control for the most part. It had become a passion. It was his raison d'etre.

The man in the brimmed hat got up from his seat and turned so that his back was to Franklin's unforgiving stare. The man could sense that Franklin was burning inside with curiosity. It was unlike him to accept anything he was told at face value. The man stepped away from the table and looked around the room. The light was dim and the silence made each of them uncomfortable. Franklin was afraid to swallow because he knew they would hear it.

"There is a person that we will want eliminated," the man in the hat began. "You must make it clear to the assigned party that this person must be killed specifically as we dictate."

The Assassination Race (Secrets of The Afterlife Society)

"The time and place of the assignment will be provided to you within a short time after the race. It will have to be carried out within hours after assigned. The location will be precise and there are to be no mistakes." The man's tone was as severe and as sharp as his demands. He turned on one heel to face Franklin again. "I can give you part of the instructions now. He or she is to be shot once in the head and, with that one shot, the target must die."

Franklin folded his manicured hands and leaned forward giving his utmost attention. They now had his full interest.

"The target will then, most likely, have to have a part of his or her body removed as quickly and as cleanly as possible. It will then have to be wrapped and secured for transport to a specific location that will be disclosed to you when we contact you again with the rest of the details."

Franklin sat perfectly still, burning the instructions into his memory. These people had been responsible for his success and he knew that they could ruin him just as easily. He had been involved with important covert operations in the past and had gained a reputable resume of accolades for his sinister achievements. The more pleased his investors were, the more he received in funding for his personal expenses. "You think there will be a body part to remove? It sounds like you aren't too sure about that ... or quite sure about the identity of your target."

Although personally wealthy, Franklin viewed himself as a generous, selfless man and donated a great amount of time to organizing The Assassination Race for the elite to have fun with. He took great pleasure in providing these men, and alien diplomats, with a private sport to place wagers on. His games were more tantalizing than any other event he could think of. On the human side, only the *crème* of the upper crust could enter their bets. They had to be connected to a secret society or a lodge deemed worthy enough to merit participation. His race was an open forum where the men, and powerful women, of various secret sects could inter-mingle with one another, setting their political and financial agendas aside for one evening a month and have some good old-fashioned fun. Franklin even donated some of the proceeds to charity. The aliens enjoyed it on a much deeper level, but they too were known to love gambling.

In Franklin's eyes, he was the Jesus of drag racing. He preached for unity amongst members. The better they all got along, the more money he made from them. He had worked hard to establish his meetings and subsequent races as a neutral ground. He was quick to learn that men of various societies didn't always get along and that after a few drinks some of them down right hated each other. To make things easier, attendance was optional. Franklin had contrived a system for accepting private bets securely online, with the help of his contacts from within the government, of course.

"That is all we have for you at this time," the white-haired man wheezed. "The identity of your target will be revealed after the race. Our contacts gave us very little to go on. We don't know the identity of the target because ... we are still waiting for something to happen first. We appreciate your hospitality, but we must be going."

"I understand, gentlemen," Franklin replied.

Franklin jumped from his seat and opened the door for the three men as they prepared to leave. He understood their instructions. And as far as they knew, his loyalty was set in stone.

Alone in the small room, he picked up the tray he had set aside earlier and neatly cleared the empty glasses from the table. Planning for the next race would not have to be altered too much. He only had to keep himself ready at any moment for contact from his nameless superiors. After the race, he would pull aside the heads of the two teams competing and let them know that things would be a little different. It would be more interesting for everyone involved.

10

Mike leapt into Edward's office, suffering the effects of a caffeine buzz. Edward stopped what he was doing, one hand suspended in mid-air holding a stapler and in the other, the papers he was about to staple. Edward smiled at Mike and wondered for a moment how caffeine could have such an effect on Mike's personality but do nothing for him.

"Hey!" Mike said. "Let's get some lunch."

Edward completed his stapling and sifted through the cluster of papers on his desk. "I can't. I have some research to do and some model I have to come up with based on some statistics I found ..."

"Blah, blah, blah," Mike laughed. He shrugged his shoulders and smiled. "Big deal. Let's get sandwiches."

Edward smirked at Mike's carefree attitude and then went back to the business of shuffling papers about.

Mike rolled his eyes and then let out an intentionally loud sigh. "I think I'm becoming allergic to you," he complained.

"Mike, I have things to do here and ..." Edward stopped short before he could finish as his eyes became distracted by Deidra walking into his office.

"Am I interrupting?" she asked.

"No," Edward said.

"I was wondering if we could get some lunch," she asked and then looked at Mike who was doing his best to sneer at her without getting caught.

"He's really busy," Mike told her.

Edward crumpled his papers into an unorganized stack and stood abruptly. "Yes, that would be nice," he blushed. He knew he was a victim when she came around. It was awkward to be so weak in front of Mike but he couldn't help it. Deidra caught him off guard when she arrived at his office door. She had been away for the past week visiting her parents in California.

"I thought you had a lot of important stapling to do," Mike teased.

Edward's face boiled with heat. He moved around to the front of his desk and slapped Mike on the back. "I'll get sandwiches with you tomorrow, sweetie," he said to him with a smile.

Deidra drove them away from the downtown business district and onto Interstate 35 going toward Waco. They had escaped the tall buildings that Edward sometimes thought of playfully as dinosaurs that would come to life and eat people in suits. Edward sat peacefully as she drove, wondering what kind of out-of-the-way restaurant she was taking them to. They seemed to drive on and on until the dino-buildings turned into tiny little building blocks that couldn't harm anyone.

He could not keep his mouth shut any longer. "Where are we going?" he asked.

"You are taking the rest of the day off. Mr. Bennett wants me to look at a car near Waco," she told him. "I thought you might want to come along."

Edward felt a tension headache coming on suddenly as he imagined the workload on his desk increasing and his email inbox filling up in his absence. "I have a lot of work to do. There's that presentation coming up and I haven't even made the charts yet!"

"Eddie, you need to relax. Mr. Bennett knows you're here with me. We have to pick out a car for the next race. That's more important than 'work,'" she informed him.

"Mr. Bennett doesn't care if I finish my work on the presentation?"

Deidra laughed, throwing her head back in the process. "No! He's not going to have people overloading you with ..." she stopped briefly to remove both hands from the steering wheel to draw quotation marks into the air before her, " 'important projects,'" she said. "The race is where he focuses his attention. Especially now. We've been in the last four in a row. We're on a winning streak."

Edward sat quietly and allowed what she told him to render into a picture in his head. It was a picture of him, sitting at his desk performing a job that was meaningless. He came to the realization that his big office, his cherry wood desk, and grand view of the Dallas sky had been handed to him for being a member of a secret club. He still didn't even know what it was called or if it had a name at all.

Deidra turned up the volume on her CD player and started moving herself around in her seat to some 80s hair metal. She drove an Audi, which confused him since as far as he knew she was Mr. Bennett's assistant. Edward tried not to let his ego bruise too badly. Maybe he *had* been given his new job because he was 'brought in'. It was still better than being killed. When he thought about it, he actually owed a lot to Deidra for saving his life.

"So nothing I've been doing at work matters?"

Deidra paused mid-head bang and looked at him. "Of course it does. What I meant was that whatever project you are working on at work is always going to be second to preparations for the race after the fifteenth of each month. I'm sure that he's got Anthony finishing up whatever you were working on."

"But it's *my* work!" Edward declared with a crazed look in his eyes.

"Geez, Eddie! You'll get credit for it!" She shook her head at him like he was a child and began mumbling under her breath, "Anthony doesn't give a shit about getting credit for some stupid-ass chart ... draw it in crayons ... nobody gives a fuck anyway ..."

Edward pouted. "That's not the point." He sank down into his seat and folded his arms. "All that work I did in college ... I looked for a job for years. All I had to do was shoot a guy and join some cult ..."

"You're such a baby," she smiled.

Edward picked himself up and forced a smile on his face. He was going to go along with the madness since he didn't seem to have any real choice in the matter. Even if his hours of toiling on the computer were, in the end, meaningless—he was going to produce the best bunch of meaningless work of his life for that company.

"What are we going to look at?" he tried asking optimistically.

Deidra's eyes lit up at the change of subject and turned down the music. "You won't believe what we found," she beamed.

Edward couldn't imagine the next monstrosity that she would be racing for Corpotex. "Another hearse?"

"No! A 1933 Rolls-Royce Phantom II!" she gasped.

Edward's face was still. "Sounds old."

"That's the point. It's cool because it's old and it looks crazy! Can you envision me in one of those? A Rolls ... sweet, right?" She was ecstatic. "It does need some work. I just take a look at it to see how much rust it has, then if the body is decent enough, I say yes, send a picture of it to Mr. Bennett with my camera, and then he has it delivered to the shop where it gets hooked up with everything it needs for the race. Of course, I'll do a few test runs when they're finished with it."

"Are there any rules to picking out these cars you guys race?" he asked.

"Yes. They have to be a hard find, and somewhat unique. Each team has to rebuild most of it from scratch. That's the hardest part. There may be some working parts still in this thing, but we have to look at them all, order what we need ... you always have to overhaul the engine or drop a new one in," she spoke with true love of the process. "Also, the two cars raced against each other have to be fitted with similar specs. So one won't have an unfair advantage over the other. The mechanics and bosses deal with that part. Negotiations ... weighing the cars' bodies for the right engine ... Oh, and there's qualifying paperwork ... geez, Anthony does a lot of that on our side."

Edward watched how animated her face became as she talked about it. The car was a forgotten shell that she would save and bring back to life. In some other dimension, old broken-down cars probably worshiped her.

"Why does this all begin after the fifteenth?" Edward asked.

"The race is on the first Friday of the month, so we need time to prepare. The two competing teams are chosen using some average that they created based upon the stock market. We're informed on the 15th if we qualify. Of course, we won last time, so we race no matter what. Our company's stock has been pretty high. But, if we lose, we can't qualify to race again for two racing periods."

"Oh," Edward replied.

"But the real reason I brought you on this trip was to discuss something that's been bothering me. I know you don't care about cars," Deidra pointed out.

"Cars are cool. What makes you think that I don't like cars? I don't know much about cars, but ... what did you want to talk about?" he asked while nervously trying to cover his ignorance about cars. "Are you in love with me?" he wished jokingly.

Deidra glared at him for a second and then lost the curve of her smile. His humor played a sour note against her thoughts and he didn't know that it had been bad timing for it. "I think

I know something about this race and I don't know who to talk to about it. I asked Mr. Bennett if I could bring you with me because I knew he would say yes, since you're in, and also because my car is clean. Not bugged," she sounded concerned.

"Am I the right person to talk to about something like this? It sounds important," he had very recently learned to have reservations about being let in on things. Secret things. The more he knew, the more he would be involved.

"You don't want me to tell you?" she asked.

"I don't know," he thought about it. Everything was coming at him so fast and the information he was being given was all linked to something illegal. He was being forced to internalize the kinds of things that people would be killed over if somehow leaked on the outside. Things *he* could be killed for. He was almost offended that Deidra wanted to endanger his life even further with something that she felt could only be discussed in a car driving away from Dallas. "You can tell me, but I can hardly keep up with the things I know already," he warned.

Deidra shook her head. "Forget it."

"Don't do that. You can tell me," he pushed. Human curiosity overwhelmed his primal need to protect himself from danger and his sexual desires for her told his brain to submit. "I just can't guarantee I will understand, that's all."

"Well, this you will understand," she cautioned, her voice a reflection of the ill-omened news she carried with her.

"Go ahead," he said while he braced himself for some kind of insanity.

"I think the loser of this next race is going to be doing more than just killing some housewife," she said matter-of-factily.

"*Just* killing a housewife?" he mumbled.

"I'm serious. I know what Franklin is like before a race," her eyes glazed over in recollection. "He's funny, and talkative. He's usually happy."

Edward saw it and sank. Her eyes revealed it to him instantly. A knot formed inside his chest and he battled with his psyche to move past it emotionally, but he couldn't. The knot unraveled itself and the disappointment spilled out of his mouth before he could control it. "You're sleeping with Franklin!"

Deidra's jaw dropped and she was speechless for a moment before reacting. "So what?" she defended herself.

"I can't believe this!" Edward exploded. "I just can't believe it!"

"The only reason you can't believe it is because you want to fuck me, too! That's the only reason you got dragged into this whole thing!" she yelled.

With that, Edward was silenced and stared out through the window. He focused on the painted line on the side of the road and watched it and the dried-out trees scattered behind it race past with the exaggerated motion of a cartoon. *She's right*, he thought. *Lucky Franklin. Dammit!*

"Eddie," she spoke softly. "My personal relationship with Franklin is my business, not yours."

Edward was steaming, but he knew that she was right. It hurt him. He held back the childish feelings of self-pity and tried to remember what it was to be a man. It was not the time to open the door to reveal security issues with his manhood. This revelation certainly didn't help his feelings of self-doubt. It seemed that everything he longed for deeply had always been out of reach for him. And being forced to face this sort of rejection once again only supported another theory he had recently developed; his standards were too high and thus he was doomed to be set up for failure.

If there was a person he could blame for his lack of self-esteem, it would be his mother. She had never dated and there was no mention of his father. The only men he knew, or even slightly admired, had been on television. When he was a kid, he wished that Magnum P.I. was his dad. Although he wasn't much of a father figure, at least he had a cool mustache. "Are you in love with him or …?"

"Or what? Or am I a slut?" she finished for him.

"No, that's not what I was going to say," his voice was gentle in defeat. He didn't want to be a sore loser.

"You were just going to imply it," she snapped.

"Deidra," he sighed. "You're right. It is not my business." He tried to brave his curiosity about the nature of their relationship and move beyond its evil nagging in his brain. He then silently blamed his mother for his emotional turbulence. "What did you learn about the race?" He looked at her again, trying to prove that he could be mature.

Deidra cleared her throat and remained focused on driving as it began to rain. "I think they're going to do something different. Franklin … talks in his sleep," she said carefully, knowing that Edward was hurt by the news of her relationship with him. She had learned to recognize the way men turned into wolves around her, but was sympathetic to it. She knew they couldn't help being bossed around by their penises. "A few nights ago he said something about shooting someone and that it was a 'big job.' He was dreaming and said, 'I won't let you down,' over and over. Then the next morning, when I mentioned the race, he said he didn't want to talk about the race," she explained.

Edward remained perfectly still. He believed her when she told him that she was going to be in California visiting her parents. She had been absent from work for a week. Now he wasn't so sure. *A few nights ago?*

"You don't understand. He loves that race. He makes a lot of money off of it but it's also his life," she added.

"Is it because he looks like Cary Grant?"

"What?"

"I used to watch his movies when I was a kid. My mom loved that guy," Edward paused. "Does Franklin know he looks like him?"

"Yes, he knows." Deidra rolled her eyes.

"I'm sorry. So what do you think is going on with the race?" Edward asked, painfully fighting the thoughts of Deidra sleeping in Franklin's mansion. He had never seen his mansion, or even knew if one existed. But now he was imagining that one existed and that Deidra had been inside it, naked.

"I think they're going to kill someone really, really important. Like a political figure or something like that."

"Like the President?" Edward guessed in horror.

"What?" she roared with laughter. "The President? He's not important!" She couldn't stop laughing. "Oh, Eddie, you are so funny. You really think that they would put the power of the whole country in the hands of one man that is elected every four years?"

"Yes?" he questioned himself.

"You probably still think we landed on the moon in the 1960s, too! *Before* cell phones!" she laughed. "No ... I think that they are going to kill someone more important than that," she stated.

Edward's head was tingling. "Who's more important than the President?" he asked.

"Lots of people," she said firmly. "Which reminds me ... after this we have a meeting tonight."

"For real work or for fake work?" Edward asked with a sarcastic grin.

"With Franklin," she answered, not understanding what Edward considered to be fake or real. "It might help you to get your mind off a few things."

"Like what?" he scoffed. "The moon?"

"Like your report and, I don't know ... just things."

11

"How is this supposed to help me get my mind off things?" Edward asked as he glanced around the dark strip club. Cigarette smoke hung heavy in the poorly ventilated air and he could make out the silhouettes of lap dancers in a far off corner, gyrating dramatically for their clients.

"I was told we needed to be here." Deidra reached into her handbag as they sat upon a few wobbly stools at the bar. "Franklin said he's entertaining some guests from out of town. This whole 'being here' thing ... is not really for your benefit. I just thought you might relax for a few minutes in the process and stop being so ... pissed off."

Embarrassed, Edward shook his head and mumbled, "Nothing ever is for me. Nothing new there."

Deidra scanned the room for Franklin and cursed wildly about not being able to find her goddamned cell phone so that she could call him to find out where he was. Neon lights, black lights, and the hot glow of an occasional cigarette was all she had to assist her in her search as she glanced across the room. She went on grumbling under her breath about why she had to carry so many things in her handbag that she didn't even need.

She slammed a fist into her handbag and looked up, realizing suddenly that everyone around them had a drink. She was willing to set her search aside for some alcohol and raised a finger to signal the bartender, but then stopped herself.

"No way," she gasped and leaned forward in her seat. Her eyes studied the bartender, taking in every detail from head to toe.

"What?" Edward asked.

"He's an intern!"

"A what?"

"Jesus, Eddie! I can't explain everything to you every second!" She fumbled around now with fury in her handbag only to piss herself off even more at not finding her cell phone again. She then slammed her fist onto the bar top and waited with a proud smirk as the bartender finished mixing a drink and approached. "This is going to be classic."

The bartender stood in front of her and nodded.

"I would like," she hung on the impending order with great pleasure. "a Pina Colada."

Edward felt as confused as he ever had with her. "Seems a bit fruity for you."

"Yes! And loud!"

The bartender smiled and waited for Deidra to stop gloating before informing her in a flat tone, "Our blender is broken."

She laughed a much exaggerated and forced laugh.

"Oh, of course it is!" She chuckled. "Well, I know they must have one in the kitchen. Why don't you go in there and borrow it so I can have my nice, cold Pina Colada."

The bartender shrugged and then looked around the room. "I'm too busy right now. Another guy called in sick. How about a Cosmo?"

"Fuck your old-lady Cosmo and make me a Pina Colada before I slap that fake-ass mustache off your face!" Deidra insisted with a scowl.

Edward was learning very quickly that Deidra had no patience for anything. She was hot-tempered and full of some kind of psychopathic fire. This didn't help him at all in the lust department as her anger somehow turned him on. But he wasn't the type of guy to just sit around like a boob when someone was being berated over a frozen drink topped with a cherry. Even if the one doing the berating was a hot chick he wanted to impress.

"Deidra, give the guy a break! It's packed in here. Just get a beer!"

"Eddie!" She swung around in her seat so fast that even with the blaring sounds of eighties metal over the sound system, he could hear the intense squeal the seat made as it swiveled in his direction. "Go stare at some fake tits or something! I want a fucking PINA COLADA!"

The bartender let out an exaggerated sigh, pursed his lips together, and relented. "Yes, ma'am."

Deidra smiled and sat up tall and proud as the bartender left his post to make his way toward the kitchen in defeat. She perked up even more and widened her eyes as he entered the kitchen's double doors.

"Happy now?" Edward asked. "He's going to spit in it ... at the very least."

"Lesson one ... watch his face when he turns the blender on," she replied with a smirk.

"Why?"

"Because interns hate the sound of a sudden, loud, intrusive noise. Chainsaws, hammers, lawn mowers, and blenders. It irritates them."

"I don't understand," Edward said, realizing within the same moment that he actually didn't want to understand.

She leaned in to his ear and whispered, "He's an alien."

Uncomfortable with the idea that Deidra may be more insane than he already had suspected, Edward decided to let it go. To just agree with her from now on about everything was beginning to sound like the best idea he had come up with all day. Perhaps the best idea of the week. He could only imagine how much smoother things would have gone for him thus far had he just agreed with her all along about everything. Things would have gone a lot smoother with all of the women that had ever entered his life if he had just realized that sooner.

"Alright, Deidra."

"They send them here to observe and study. This one is posing as a bartender," she went on to explain. "Think about it. What is a better way to learn about the perverted minds of men, the so-called 'dominant species,' than to listen to their moronic, drunken babbling as they waste all their money on the true dominant species, the ever-tantalizing human female."

Edward shifted in his seat as he saw the bartender returning from the kitchen with a large blender.

"Okay, he's an alien. Shhhhhh." Edward did his best to return to normal. He rearranged himself in his seat to make sure that the bartender had no idea that he had just been discussing his alien internship on Earth with his demanding lady friend.

The bartender placed the blender down on the bar top and plugged it in. He stopped to take in a deep breath before grabbing a bottle of rum and the Pina Coloda mixer. He poured them both in. The bartender then looked straight at Edward. Edward smiled uneasily, as if trying to convey the sympathy he felt for the poor man forced into a strange form of frozen-drink-making submission. Then the bartender turned back to his task and turned the blender on.

The bartender's face went into an array of horribly contorted expressions. Holding the blender's button down sent electric jolts through his arm. The man's agony appeared to intensify even as the blades of the machine chopped the ice cubes into smaller, less challenging pieces. His teeth clenched and his eyes rolled back. With his free hand, he gripped an ear and pushed hard against his head. His lips trembled violently as saliva ran freely from his mouth. And then the blender went silent and the bartender slumped over in exhaustion, grabbing ahold of the countertop with shaking arms to keep himself from falling over.

The man straightened his posture and with a stiff smile in Deidra's direction, poured the white, frosty drink into a tall glass before topping his painful creation with a cherry.

Deidra watched as the now extremely annoyed bartender placed a cardboard coaster in front of her and set the drink down with a hard slam. Deidra looked very pleased with herself, and the obnoxious drink.

"No straw?"

A man across the room suddenly caught Edward's attention as he repeatedly swung his arms above his head. It was Franklin except a bit drunker and more jovial than he expected him to be for someone on a supposed business meeting. Franklin flashed a wide smile at catching Edward's attention and held up a shot glass in celebration.

Edward tapped Deidra on the shoulder and pointed. "I think he wants us to sit with him."

Deidra spun around in her seat and squinted at the man she thought most resembled Franklin, then turned to Edward.

"Brace yourself," she warned in a deep voice.

He shook his head and waited for the next installment of Deidra's lesson in paranoia.

"Oh no!" Edward began dramatically. "He's not really Franklin, is he? He's an alien!"

"You know what, asshole?" Deidra's voice was elevated. The anger she felt caused her to shake, but she was still able to take a large gulp from the strawless frozen drink in her hand before continuing. "I could have killed you that day."

"What? In the Hearse? With your driving?" Edward teased. He glanced back at the bartender for a moment and wondered why he was licking a used pint glass with a piece of gum stuck to the bottom.

"No. I didn't want to bring you in," she declared loudly. "I can't stand training ignorant fucks like you. College boys, frat boys, mamas' boys ... all brought into this world and put in front of a TV to watch reruns, corporate bullshit commercials, and learn everything about the world through a bought and sold media machine!"

In his peripheral vision, Edward watched the bartender place an olive into his eye, pushing it all the way into the socket.

"I swear on my mother's grave that if you only knew half of what I know about this planet you would run home and grab your fucking teddy bear like a little bitch ..."

At that point, Deidra's words trailed off. As much as he didn't want to hear about how stupid she rightfully thought he was, Edward also did not want to be anywhere near the bartender. He grabbed Deidra's arm and began to walk them both toward Franklin. She stopped in her tracks.

"What the hell? Did you hear anything I said, frat boy?"

Now at a safer distance, Edward peaked back to see if the bartender noticed him leaving so hastily. The bartender smiled, waved, and winked his olive eye at Edward.

"Christ!"

"Did you hear me?" She yelled in his face.

"Jesus Christ, Yes!" Edward yelled back in horror. "Yes!"

"Because I have something else to tell you and you had better pay attention or I'm going to let Franklin know that I volunteer to be the one to put the bullet in your head when you fuck up and get us all in trouble for not listening to me!"

"Yes, I'm listening, but I am just so ready to go sit with Franklin now. I'm ready to sit with him now. Please. Now. Okay?" Edward was sure to keep his back to the bar while he did his best to control his breathing.

"Franklin is sitting with a group of extremely important diplomats. Racing investors. If you act like an ignorant shithead, I am sure that Franklin will finally let me kill you." She sneered.

"If you really wanted me dead, you wouldn't be giving me tips on how not to get dead." Edward was simply unable to refrain from pushing her buttons when it just seemed so easy.

Deidra's eyes nearly popped out of her head. "Shut up."

"So, what do I do?"

"You sit there and drink. You say nothing and think about nothing."

"Okay."

"I'm serious!"

"I know! Believe me, I think I'm starting to get it," he stammered as he resisted the urge to take another peak at what the bartender was up to.

She grabbed his arm and led them to Franklin's cozy table near the darkest corner of the room. Deidra had just enough time to run her fingers through the back of her hair in a quick style adjustment before catching Franklin's eye and smiling. She leaned in to Edward, pretending to brush some dandruff from his shoulder.

"They're aliens."

"Who? What? The Diplomats?" he complained.

"Yeah. Now you have the next two seconds to get over it and empty your thoughts."

"Oh."

Edward couldn't breathe. Over a few heart palpitations, he thought about how it was a running theme of aliens everyplace he went. He needed a break. An alien-free vacation. And now, he had to mingle with them, or not. He wasn't too sure what was expected of him. He didn't have control over his own life anymore and now Deidra was telling him how to think as well.

He remembered having a plan once. It involved working in a cubicle and having a decent benefits package. He wanted a hot meal once in a while and envisioned having a girlfriend that was willing to put out. But for now, he was shaking hands with an alien that looked like a human with a botched face lift.

"My dear friends," Franklin smiled and looked warmly at his guests. "This is the young man I was telling you about, Edward!"

Edward forced something that resembled a smile, but found it hard to make eye contact with any of the fake eyes looking back at him. He took his seat next to Franklin as quickly as possible. He then looked to Deidra for guidance. She was still standing, but with both eyes tightly shut. He knew that she was someplace else entirely, cleaning her mind of all thought. This was her tin foil helmet face.

"Edward, my friends here are very interested in what you think is entertaining."

"I ... well," Edward stammered.

"Anything that comes to mind," Franklin pressed while snapping his fingers to help speed things along.

Edward mustered up enough courage to look up and away from his nervous hands and into the empty glass eyes of his questioners.

"Can ... um ... can I have a beer?"

"Of course!" Franklin chuckled. "Deidra?"

Deidra opened her eyes and let out a long breath before heading for the bar as fast as she could.

The aliens stared at Edward, intrigued with the possibilities his human mind presented.

"Um, I like going to the movies," he told them calmly.

"Well that's nice," Franklin agreed half-heartedly. "With the popcorn and the dirty floors ... you are just sitting there watching a contrived concoction of bad acting, editing, and ... what about skiing or sky diving?"

"I'm more of just a sitter, I guess." Edward felt more generic than ever.

The alien diplomats stared at Franklin. The blank looks in their faces scared Edward.

"Eddie," Franklin began in that fatherly tone he kept throwing at him from time to time. "There must be something that you like to do that ignites that spark within you. Maybe something as simple as a good book. Reading! We love to read! Right?"

The diplomats all turned to Edward for a response. It was his turn to speak. To communicate verbally with his fellow human counterpart. To agree with Franklin about books while at the same time unable to remember the last time he actually picked one up. He knew that he was being studied by them. They wanted him to express his innermost passions and be okay with it. Even with the stretched plastic faces, he could tell that they were eager to listen, desperate to learn from him what they could. And even though he was beginning to feel like a sideshow freak, he wished that he wanted to participate but just didn't know anything significant enough to say.

"I like ladies. Nice ones. Not ones that boss you around and put you down all the time …"

Franklin smiled contently. The diplomats leaned in unison toward Franklin and stared into his eyes until his facial expression crinkled and his head began to nod in some sort of agreement.

"Eddie?" Franklin asked.

"Yes?"

"They want to know about your other interest."

Edward looked for Deidra but could not see her anywhere through the cancerous cloud of smoke surrounding their table. She was still getting his drink order and most likely harassing the bartender in the process.

"What other interest? Oh, like food?" he guessed, trying not to look too long into any of the diplomats faces.

"Uh, no, Eddie. They seem a bit more interested in your more personal activities," Franklin stopped to take a peanut from a small bowl in front of him. "Sex."

Edward squirmed in his seat. "I haven't had sex for, I don't know … two years?"

Franklin shot up in his seat. "That's fucking insane! Are you serious?"

Edward, having the full attention of the aliens, Franklin, and a nosey man seated at the next table who felt that Edward's sex life was more interesting than the conversation his table was having about the Canadian healthcare system, felt his face get hot. "No. No. No sex for the past two years. No big deal."

"You do enjoy it, right?" Franklin queried.

"Yes."

"Would you say that you enjoy it more than other things?"

Edward glared at the man at the next table, hoping to remind him of his manners by doing so, but failed. "Yes."

"More than sports?"

"Yes."

"More than fishing?"

"I don't fish."

"More than candy?"

"Uh, yes."

"Then why aren't you having any? If you would like to pick a girl here, I can help you with this…"

"It's not my choice or anything," Edward explained. "I'm just not dating anyone and I'm not the prostitute type, so you know?"

The aliens leaned in toward Franklin again. Edward waited anxiously for their next humiliating brain probe and by the look on Franklin's face, it was going to be a killer.

"My friends would like to know if your interest in pornography-fueled activities is what might be keeping you from pursuing a real partner," Franklin asked with a subtle grin.

Edward, drained of all humility, closed his eyes and shook his head. He tried to empty his thoughts like Deidra told him to, but apparently that hadn't worked out. They saw right through his weak, little earth-mind with perfect clarity. He covered his eyes with his sweaty hands and sank back into his sparkly vinyl seat.

"Franklin!" Deidra protested as she approached with a beer topped with a slice of pineapple, way too many cherries, and an umbrella. "Remind your business associates to remember their Earth manners!"

Franklin's guests stopped staring at Edward and turned in unison back to their host. Like puppets, they eagerly waited for their next instruction.

"You should all look at boobies for a while. Men love doing that. It's very insightful!" Franklin praised in a chipper tone.

After taking a moment to shake their heads in agreement, the aliens took to observing the Earth females performing on the stage in front of their table. Deidra rolled her eyes at Franklin, and Edward tried as best as possible to regain his composure.

"Here, Eddie," Deidra said as she handed Edward his beer. "Sorry about all the fruit I put in there. Now I kinda feel bad."

12

The first Friday of the month.

"Are you coming home this weekend?" Edward's mother asked insecurely. She knew that he missed her. He was probably busy adjusting to his new life.

Edward's chest overflowed with guilt. "No, mom. I can't this weekend. I have too much to do," he replied.

"I know," she comforted him, and herself.

"Maybe next weekend," Edward offered.

"It's okay. Have you made any new friends there?" she asked. She knew she had to change the subject or she would cry. Everything in her world was built around her son and she never wanted to risk distancing herself from him with her overbearing emotions.

"I guess I've made a few," he replied.

"Have you met any girls?" she asked.

Edward paused to mull it over before answering, but his mother read into the silence too quickly.

"You have! What's her name?" she asked eagerly. Although she was reluctant to share her son with another woman, at least there might be a production of mini-Edwards from the right union.

"No," Edward began. "There's no girl. Mom, I have to go. I'll call you tomorrow," he needed to get off the phone. Talking about women with his mother made him feel like a goofy junior high student. *Oh yeah, mom. I met a girl, but she's mental and she's sleeping with a guy that tried to trick me into killing someone. It's okay. He's cool. He runs an illegal gambling operation and I joined it.*

Edward disconnected the call on his cell phone and looked around his office. It was Friday, casual dress day, but he still opted for a suit. If his job wasn't important, at least he would make it look like it was. Monday's presentation had been hell and the suit he had on was his only source of dignity.

The race was that evening and he had only seen Deidra once the entire day, running down the hall past his office with a cell phone attached to her ear. He felt less connected to her every day. It seemed like she was avoiding him now.

The past two weeks had been a blur. He was asked to tag along with Deidra as she made preparations for the race. Edward had become so busy acting as her assistant to work outside of fake work that he forgot all about the big presentation he was supposed to give related to real work at fake work until that Monday—the day of the presentation. His assistant Anthony threw together what he needed and shoved some cue cards into Edward's hands when he arrived that morning. Anthony told him that the visitors were already being seated in the large meeting room at the end of the hall. Edward scanned the cards anxiously for two minutes before making his way to the meeting.

As he approached the closed door, he took a breath and then entered after psyching himself up with some chant he learned from a book on meditation. He walked through the room, avoiding any real eye contact and greeted Mr. Bennett, seated near the far end of a long table. There was a laptop computer set up in the center of the table displaying stock quotes.

Mr. Bennett smiled and grasped Edward's hand firmly for a handshake. "Hello, Edward," he said with warmth.

Edward fumbled with the cards in his hand and accidentally let a few of them spill onto the burgundy carpet below. He collected them and tried to place them back in order, but realized that it was useless to fight the jests of fate.

"When am I supposed to give my presentation?" he asked weakly.

"I'll introduce you," Mr. Bennett answered back. Mr. Bennett was always kind to him. He didn't fit Edward's idea of a ruthless corporate boss. "Relax."

Edward took a seat next to Mr. Bennett and decided to wrestle with the disarrangement of cards again. When he finally had them back in order, Mr. Bennett rose from his seat.

"Good morning, gentlemen," he began. His suit was tailored perfectly on his body and the material was fresh. "Would anyone like a cup of coffee or a pastry before we begin?"

A show of nods caused Deidra to appear into Edward's view, carrying a small tray. She balanced the tray with one hand as she laid out delicate napkins with the other. She presented the tray to each man with a tilt in her hip. After a decision was made, she would then place their choice of fried flour and sugar onto the frilly napkin in front of them. Another assistant would then appear behind her with a tray of pre-filled coffee cups atop their matching saucers. The petite blonde assistant spoke in a high-pitched voice, reminding him of a flight attendant. She repeatedly asked, "Cream or sugar?" in the exact same squeaky tone to each man. Her smile tipped on the border of sadistic.

"Gentlemen," Mr. Bennett said, to set the meeting in motion. "You already know why we're here. My software is the best choice for your business solutions. You know that ... I certainly know it," he spoke with confidence. Edward listened as Mr. Bennett used one of the most intense Texas accents he had ever heard. Having lived in the Lone Star State his entire life had exposed him to a variety of southern drawls and dialects, but this one was distinct. It could have only been made in Texas, by a Texan.

"So, you are sure to be interested in my next desktop accounting product and Mr. Bloodgood here is gonna tell you what it's all about. Then ya'll can get your techie boys to install it on yer networks," Mr. Bennett flashed a broad smile at Edward. That smile was the only cue given to let him know that it was his turn to speak.

Edward banged his elbow on the edge of the table when he stood too quickly. He tried to recover by pushing his seat in extra slow. He glanced at Deidra to see her leaning against the back wall, gazing out through the slit of a mini-blind separating them from a view of cluttered buildings and strategically relocated trees.

As he made his way to the front of the room, Mr. Bennett took his seat and bit into a danish.

The charts and graphs Anthony had created less than a week before had been enlarged and placed onto pieces of oversized cardstock and positioned against two dry erase boards facing Mr. Bennett's guests. Edward stood himself inside the gap that existed between the two exaggerated representations of Corpotex market research and shuffled his feet. He then looked around the table and counted ten guests. He could feel perspiration collecting under his shirt and briefly forgot whether or not he had applied deodorant that morning. He then recalled a vision of dropping the deodorant into the toilet that he forgot to flush. *It's only under one arm.*

"Hello," Edward started out, feebly. He turned to face one of the graphs that Anthony had printed and tried to think of something to say. He was still cloudy from the beers he drank alone the night before. "Each of you have to deal with large amounts of data on a daily basis. You may be asking yourself, 'When does this data become usable information?'" Edward wanted to fake a heart attack. He pointed a shaky finger at the graph to his left and then looked out into the faces of the businessmen before him. None of them were looking at him or paying attention to him in the slightest.

Edward froze. His eyes moved around the table, watching as the men ate their pastries and sipped coffee. They texted on their phones and surfed the Internet. The table was now covered in sugary flakes and colorful sprinkles like confetti. Not one of them seemed to have noticed that Edward was practically petrified in front of them. The men continued to ignore him, enraptured with their artery-clogging treats.

Edward relaxed his ridged stance as he fixed his eyes upon a balding man that appeared to be in his late fifties. He studied the thick-rimmed glasses the guy was wearing as Edward retrieved a disturbing image that had been etched into his brain. The last time he saw that man, he was wearing a studded collar and pink vinyl pants. *That's the bitch!*

He abandoned the use of his cue cards and decided to start mumbling about increased productivity as a direct result of Corpotex software when he noticed a man at the table look up at him. Edward slipped the cards into his jacket and relinquished his brain from its duty to flood him with positive, inspirational thoughts he had requested earlier. He didn't need them to get him through the meeting any longer. Instead, he rambled on about averages and statistics while focusing in on each face in the room.

Their blatant disinterest in his presentation sobered him to the truth. Before him sat a room of moral defectives who had already agreed in advance to purchase whatever product Corpotex was willing to spew at them. The presentation was a farce and Edward was the puppet. For whatever technical reason, the fake meeting had to take place and the only ones not let in on that fact had been Edward and the dim-witted cream-or-sugar lady. She stood in the back of the room wearing a stupefied smile.

Edward turned to the graph on his left and slapped it forcefully with an open palm. "This one here is my favorite! Isn't it pretty?" he asked with a twitch in his eye. "I chose these colors because they matched the tile in the bathroom down the hall," he stopped to look at them. Only three faces reacted to his tantrum, but only out of utter boredom. One of them stopped chewing momentarily while the other two glanced at him out of habit when he hit the chart.

He tried as hard as he could to deny himself an episode of temporary insanity. Still, he continued to speak, going on and on about software. He looked across the room at Deidra, longing for her attention. As he continued speaking, he imagined throwing himself out the window. He wanted to run full-speed, smash through the glass, and fall backward so he could see the look on her face as she screamed in agony over his imminent death until he hit the sidewalk below.

He stopped speaking when she looked back at him suddenly. His words had been nothing but nonsense. She smiled and put her hand up to her mouth to hide her giggling. Edward smiled back. She was reacting to a comment he made about Corpotex making cool products that didn't suck so much.

"I guess that's all I have," Edward professed with his arms out-stretched beside him. "Any questions?" he joked with himself.

Mr. Bennett rose to his feet and applauded wildly. "Great job, Edward!" he exclaimed. "That presentation was inspiring."

Others in the room joined in. The applause was dull, but contagious. Edward walked straight out of the room and back into his office without so much as a glance from the gaggle of suits at the table.

But before Edward could erase the memory that Monday's humiliation had created, Friday was upon him without warning. *Well, except for Thursday. I guess that would be the real warning...*

"Eddie," Deidra called from his office doorway.

Edward was more than reluctant to look at her. He knew that the way she fit into her casual Friday jeans would cause him pain. He cursed himself for being superficial. It was exactly the behavior his mother had discouraged in him. She wanted him to look at a woman's intellect. "What?" he asked, pretending not to notice her.

"Mr. Bennett wants to see you," she told him. "In the garage."

Edward looked up to read the expression on her face and determined that something serious was going on. "Why? Does he want to kick my ass down there?"

Deidra smiled uncomfortably. "No. Just go see what he wants," she urged.

Edward took the stairwell down to the garage. When he opened the door, Mr. Bennett turned to Edward and smiled proudly. "There's my favorite guy!" he roared.

Edward took a few steps into the parking garage and exhaled slowly. Deidra was right. He had seen too many movies because, for a second, he thought that meeting with Mr. Bennett in the garage had all the makings of a mob hit.

"Now, Edward. Don't be upset with me if I picked out the wrong one, but surprise!" Mr. Bennett stepped aside and revealed a black Mercedes.

"I ... I don't," he stammered.

"What the hell's wrong with you?" Mr. Bennett laughed. "This car doesn't give you a hard-on?"

Edward didn't know what to think. The car was far beyond any he would have set his sights on.

"A little birdie told me to get you an automatic." Mr. Bennett was enjoying himself.

"I don't understand."

"It's for doing such a good job selling that new software at the presentation on Monday. Consider it a bonus!"

Edward couldn't keep his balance. His body lost control over his legs. They wobbled mercilessly under his body. While he was ashamed of Mr. Bennett for being a crook, he was also ready to forgive him in exchange for the so-called 'bonus'.

"I don't deserve this," Edward explained, doing his best to remain levelheaded in the face of extreme material temptation.

"Boy," Mr. Bennett said in a fatherly tone. "Take the car. Park it in your parking space, and keep doing whatever it is you do in that office of yours."

Edward had to think fast as Mr. Bennett tossed the car keys up into the air in his direction. They landed in his hands with a sweet jingle. Mr. Bennett patted him on the shoulder as he moved past him to head toward his Jag.

He stood in the presence of his new car, unsure of what to do next. He was tempted to get inside and smell its pristine interior, but resisted. Instead, he turned away from it in fear.

He wouldn't know how to handle himself if greed took over. He closed his eyes and realized that between his thumb and fingers, he was caressing the keys in his grasp. He wanted the car. *It's mine*, he thought. *I own it*.

"Wow," Deidra said into the side of his face.

Edward opened his eyes, startled. He didn't hear her approach at all.

"Are you going to take me to lunch in that?" she eyed the car's body with interest and ran her finger over the hood.

"Uh, sure," he replied. "I guess I could do that."

"Well, let's go," she insisted.

13

Edward looked across the table at her and watched as she picked at her pasta. She patiently moved aside large chunks of garlic onto the rim of her dish. The oversized fork in her hand looked comical to him. Whenever she twirled it to gather long strands of vermicelli, the pieces would slip through the fork's extra wide teeth.

"They put way too much olive oil in this," she said in frustration.

"Are you ready for tonight?" he asked.

"Yes."

"Any new developments?" he looked at her differently to signal that he was asking as discreetly as possible about her concerns with that night's race.

Deidra put her fork down and clutched the cloth napkin on her lap. "Actually, yes."

Edward leaned in. "Can you talk about it?" he asked in a hushed voice.

"I don't know," she began. "I guess I only told you before because I felt guilty for bringing you into all of this, but now I just don't want to bother you with it," she spoke into her lap while kneading the napkin with her fingers.

"You're not bothering me. If you don't want to tell me, I'll understand."

Deidra looked up at him with tears gleaming in her eyes. Her eyes sparkled in the soft light of the restaurant and her face was flush. She inhaled a deep breath and let go of it carefully. She refused to allow herself to cry and he could see the color in her face returning to normal as she struggled to gain back her composure.

"If I tell you, you can't get upset," she warned him.

Edward knew what she meant. She was going to discuss what she had learned, but Franklin was involved and she didn't want him to be jealous.

"Okay," he agreed.

"Last night, we were about to, you know," she began. "But his phone rang. He went into another room to answer it and then after a few minutes he came back into his bedroom and started putting his clothes back on."

Edward was busy putting a lot of pressure on his brain to keep a neutral expression on his face. He didn't want to think about Franklin defiling Deidra in the least. And in recent weeks, it came to his attention that he had less control over his own mind than he had originally thought. When people made their way into his office to discuss work matters, he would drift off into a void he had created like some empty folder on his computer desktop.

He exerted great influence over his eyebrow muscles as he listened to her. She was the type to read his face as she spoke. She did this to gauge his true understanding of things she discussed. He was doing his best to make her believe he could remain neutral about her relationship. Still, he was aware that at any given time, his face muscles could revolt against him and ruin all of his deceptive work.

Deidra studied him for a reaction before continuing. "I tried to get him interested again, but he couldn't," she said. She was pulling on the ends of her sleeves near her wrists. It was a nervous habit he noticed about her.

Edward played the part of a friend, trying not to overdo his sincerity. "Did he say anything about the call?"

"No. And he told me that I had to leave." The tears tried to force their way out of her tear ducts, but she wouldn't let them go. "He was mean about it, too," she added with a sniffle.

"I'm sorry," he said painfully.

"He told me that there were more important things in life than sex. I was offended because to me, it's not just sex." She looked down at her lunch and let out a quivering sigh. "He called me a whore."

Edward didn't know how to comfort her. Horrible thoughts entered his head. He looked down at her hands again, resting on the edge of the table top. He watched as she fumbled endlessly with her sleeves. He looked within himself for an honest answer. Could he be fair with his advice? He wondered suddenly if Franklin had hurt her. He wondered if she wore long sleeves and sweaters all the time to hide the bruises he gave her. He couldn't be a good friend to her. He was looking for reasons for her to leave Franklin.

"Eddie, I don't have any real friends. Women usually have other girls they go out with. I don't. I can't. I've never discussed my relationship with Frankie to anyone." She placed her napkin over her food and took a drink of water. "It's like we don't exist."

"Do you love him?" Edward lost the war with his brain and had to ask.

Deidra looked at him. She traced every detail of his face with her eyes. When she connected with his pupils again, her eyes dilated. "No."

Edward breathed again.

"It's based on admiration. I find him fascinating, but only up to a point. He tells me that I'm beautiful. He says that if I had been alive during the time of the Masters, I would have been immortalized by them. He says that they would have sought me out to paint me," she trailed off. "He is a beautiful man in so many ways. Except when it comes to love, or his feelings for me … I know that he just says those things to lure me in. He knows how alone I feel in the world. He doesn't want a wife or love. I understood that from the beginning and I thought I could handle it, but it hurts now."

"Do you ever talk about that? Do you two ever have real talks about anything?" he asked.

"Just about the news or the race. And sometimes about … well," she glanced around the room before leaning in across the table. "Sometimes he tells me about this thing he wants to do with some of his money someday. He doesn't really have anyone to leave it *all* to and after a few drinks sometimes he talks about—don't laugh … an alien racing project that he wants to set up. I don't know … nothing else significant though. I think he tries to keep me around by treating me to vacations whenever I want. That way we can talk about the scenery or the food, not each other. Distractions."

"Doesn't it make you feel bad? No real conversations?" Edward asked, knowing what the answer would be.

"No," she looked around to make sure their waiter wasn't coming over and then whispered to herself, "What does it matter? Have you ever been in love?"

"I don't think so," he answered honestly.

She looked past him and smiled. "I wrote this guy a letter once telling him how I felt." She looked down into her lap again. "We had so much in common and there was this connection that we had … he made me smile. Just being around him made me feel high. I know he felt the same way. I could see it in his eyes … ice blue. People's eyes can tell you everything."

"Where is he?"

She looked at his empty glass and then into his eyes. "He's out there somewhere. I see him around sometimes. He never spoke to me again after the letter. Telling people how you feel is a bad idea. It's better to just take what is handed to you in life sometimes and focus on yourself."

"Did you love him?"

"Deeply. I'll probably never feel anything like that again. But I learned my lesson from it."

He stared at her blankly and pushed the thought of her wasting her time with Franklin out of his mind. Then he had to force himself not to ask if Franklin was hitting her. Edward wanted to take her by the hand and say something to empower her, but he couldn't. It would all come out sounding selfish anyway.

"Maybe he's just stressed out about whatever is going on with this next race," she thought out loud.

Edward panicked. "No! Deidra, you can't let him treat you like this. Don't try and justify what he's done ... or how he treats you."

She was quiet for a few seconds and then sat up straight. "You're right. I'm not going home with him tonight," she said strongly.

"Good!" Edward praised.

"And I don't care what he says to try and seduce me," she stated adamantly. "You know, one time he had my car filled with roses because I didn't call him for a week."

Edward scoffed sarcastically. "That's original."

She stared out across the dining room and frowned. "None of these people know," she said under her breath.

"Know what?"

"Why they work so much. Why they have so much debt. They don't know who really owns them," she replied faintly.

"What do you mean?" he asked.

"Nothing," she dismissed. "I have to get home and pick out something cool to wear for tonight. What are you wearing?" she asked with excitement. Her face suddenly filled with electricity at the change of topic.

Edward looked down at himself, stumped. "I'm wearing this?"

"A suit?" she laughed. "Come on, you have to do better than that. Be more adventurous."

He marveled at her enthusiasm. Her mood swings could have been classified as dangerous, but he didn't care. "What do you suggest?"

She contemplated briefly. "How about a disco dancer?"

Edward recoiled. "Yuck."

"Well, I don't know. I'm going 1930s tonight. It's kind of on purpose. You know … to match the car," she said. "Some of what we do is set up a certain way. Like a part of a plan."

"Hmmmm. I think I'll just go as a stupid guy from Corpotex," he joked with a straight face.

Deidra smiled. "I have to ask you a favor."

"What?"

"If I have too much to drink tonight and look like I'm getting sad, please remind me not to give in to him."

Edward wasn't sure how far he would go to stop her and he definitely didn't want Franklin to be upset with him for getting involved. "I'll try."

14

Edward waited, parked outside Deidra's apartment gate. It took her almost 40 minutes to get ready and then drive through to meet him. She hadn't told him earlier that they would be riding separately to the meeting.

She let her window down as she stopped beside him. "Just follow me," she said to him after he took too many seconds to find the right button to let his window down.

"Why don't we just go in one car?" he asked.

"I don't think that would look good," she responded.

Through her car window, he could see that her hair had been styled differently. She closed her window and began to drive ahead of him but waited, watching in her rearview mirror. She was waiting on him to follow her.

He hoped to have her as a passenger in his new car again. The car intimidated him. He felt like a stranger inside of it and needed a passenger to distract him as he drove.

They went well beyond the city limits as dusk came and went. Edward could see that it was a clear night. The stars sat above, surrounding only a slice of the moon. They drove in between fields of cows that stood silently in the moonlight. Edward noticed a few of their heads turn in their direction as their cars past. The cows were probably suspicious. Edward knew that the cows had probably seen more than most people would ever figure out.

Deidra took a turn onto an unmarked road and the roads became rocky in some parts and had many dips that Edward wasn't prepared to take. He came to the conclusion that Deidra didn't slow down for anything as his car bumped and scraped against the gravel.

The road turned them in another direction and Edward could make out the faint glow of headlights moving in the distance ahead. As they got closer, he could see a number of cars parked together next to an old building that looked distinctly different from the one at the last meeting.

He watched Deidra park her car before parking his own next to hers. He got out of the Mercedes and stood behind it at its trunk, waiting patiently for her to meet him there. After patting her face with powder from her compact, she stepped out in a long, pale green dress and a black leather jacket. Her shoes were a darker green with thick heels and a rounded toe. In her hands she clutched a white beaded purse that shimmered in a variety of iridescent colors.

Edward smiled, in awe of how authentically her vintage clothing took to her. The motorcycle jacket didn't seem to match, but it looked good on her. She reminded him of a movie star from the 1930's, but couldn't remember her name. *Myrna something*, he tried to recall.

"You like it?" she asked.

"I think it looks great," he replied. "Your hair looks ... I used to watch a lot of old movies and what I'm trying to say is ... it matches perfectly!"

Deidra patted the top of her head lightly. "It's a wig," she confessed.

Edward stepped in closer to get a better look. He reached out instinctively to touch the ripples set into the black-bobbed wig, but stopped himself, hand mid-air, to read her eyes for permission. She smiled and nodded once in return.

"Wow," he said genuinely.

"Oh!" she jumped. "I almost forgot the hat!" She spun around and reached into her car to retrieve a green hat that matched her shoes. She set it on top of the wig, tilting it dramatically to her right. Its floppy brim moved in the slight breeze around them.

"Is this the same place as last time?" Edward asked while looking around himself, lost in the absence of scenery.

"No. We have to move around."

Edward walked with Deidra to join the meeting. It carried on in much the same way as before. And although the outside of the building looked more rustic than the last one, the inside was exactly the same. Edward observed many oddities as he moved through the large room. He felt trapped inside a B-movie as strange characters mingled all around. As he approached the bar alongside Deidra, he noticed a couple of zombies in deep conversation over frothy mugs of beer.

After a few drinks, a meeting took place. Franklin took to the podium in a black tuxedo, making announcements related to the organization's financial standings and then moved quickly through a proposal for the creation of a charity that would help disadvantaged youths with high IQs get into the Ivy League schools they deserved to attend. Franklin made a last call for bets and then apologized for not being as alert as usual. He was taking a new allergy medication that was making him drowsy.

Before they broke for the racetrack, Deidra ordered a chocolate martini for luck. Edward sat beside her and watched as she followed Franklin with her eyes. He stopped to make idle conversations with his guests and then he made his way toward the back exit, not once looking in her direction.

Deidra threw back her head and set the rim of the martini glass on her cherry red lips. "Whatever," she said, trying her best to put on a front. She drank the entire martini like a shot.

Edward got up to leave as a large man with a scruffy brown beard approached them and snatched Deidra's empty glass from her hand. He then smashed the glass against the bar top, causing the bartender to flinch.

"What's going on, loser?" the man asked her in a deep voice.

Edward looked straight ahead, avoiding the man's eyes. He was best described as a bearded sasquatch in a Hawaiian shirt and baggy jeans. He was well over 6 feet tall and had a large, muscular stature. The man sneered at Deidra and then broke into laughter.

"Deidra Cortez Bonaparte ... I heard about that last race!" The man tried hard to catch his breath between laughs. "I heard ... I heard your friend here screamed like a girl-baby the whole time. Is he riding with you again tonight?"

"Why do people fuck with me so much?" she asked herself before turning to face her competitor. "Listen. We've won four in a row. That's a record. You can't win."

"I don't give a fuck about any record. Corpotex is in deep shit tonight," the man growled.

Deidra grabbed Edward by the arm. "Come on. Let's go," she commanded while rolling her eyes in disgust.

The large man refused to move aside and was making a kissy face at Edward. Deidra pushed into him with her shoulder at full force until the man smiled and moved out of her way.

"What was that?" Edward was afraid to ask.

"That was Robert Crest. My competition for tonight. He's driving for Cain Computers," she answered. "They think they're bad-asses because they got some top secret programming contracts out of the government, but they are just a bunch of stupid worthless fucks."

They drove in separate vehicles again to the track. Edward followed Deidra closely. He slouched in his seat, focusing upward to scan the night sky for the mysterious helicopters to appear, but saw nothing. The long line of cars and trucks took a turn into a dark field just as expected. They drove until they reached a well-lit open area where people proceeded to park in the grass.

Edward could see bleachers facing an asphalt track. It was a replica of the one from the last race.

Near the outside of the track sat two cars. He instantly recognized the Rolls Royce, even though it had been repainted and fitted with chrome. It was a far cry from the skeletal frame he and Deidra found in Waco. He remembered how her eyes lit up when she first saw it. The other vehicle's make didn't register in Edward's brain, but it looked about as ancient as Deidra's car.

Deidra slammed her car door and rushed through the thick crowd, clutching her handbag tightly with one hand and holding down her tilted hat with the other. She moved between parked cars with her head held high. She strode past Franklin who only glanced at her briefly before finishing his conversation with another man and making his way to his seat in the bleachers.

Edward thought that he should make an effort to wish Deidra luck before she prepared to race. He knew she was distracted with thoughts of Franklin. He quickly jogged toward her and noticed her team of mechanics inspecting her car.

"Deidra," he called, out of breath.

She turned and looked away from him. Her eyes hung heavy. A man approached her with black motorcycle boots in his hands and waited as she kicked off her heels. "What?" she asked, lacking enthusiasm.

"Good luck," he answered.

After pulling up the second boot as high as she could, she straightened herself to look him in the eye. "Thanks."

The sound system crackled and the same announcer who had introduced the last race took to the microphone. "Attention, racing teams. Prepare for pre-staging. This is your 5-minute warning."

Deidra pulled off her hat and threw it into the open passenger side window while the man in the Hawaiian shirt ran across the field to his vehicle. "You should find a seat. Aren't you glad you're not riding with me this time?" Deidra asked while removing her leather jacket.

Edward grinned. "Actually, I'm a little jealous ... I ..."

He stopped speaking and his mouth dropped open.

Deidra threw her jacket into the back of a mechanic walking by and adjusted the thin straps of her dress. She pulled them up onto her shoulders and smirked at Edward quickly before looking away. "What's wrong?" she smiled.

"Nothing," he said while staring at the full sleeves of tattoos on her arms. They were bright, colorful, and perfect on her.

"Tattoos bother you?" she asked.

"No," he answered. "They are amazing ..."

"Thanks," she smiled.

"Why do you keep them hidden all the time?" he asked.

"Well, as much as I like them, it's an easy way to be noticed when you don't want to be. We don't have many friends in this business."

Edward realized now the conflict she must have felt. Part of her personality had to be kept hidden at times. It was a necessary evil in her efforts to survive the life she was involved in. To Edward, it was as if the circle of criminals she associated with had sucked away part of her soul. "I see you chose classic works of art," he smiled.

Deidra responded with distance in her eyes. He did everything he could to take his eyes off the art on her arms and when he did, he could see the frown lines in her forehead. She swallowed hard and turned her head to watch a member of her team jump into the Rolls and start up the engine. It rumbled loud and clean. "I have to go."

Edward headed for the stands, crossing the asphalt track on which the two cars were being positioned. He took a seat in the third row, sitting diagonally and to the right above Franklin and his intimate group of wealthy hooligans. Mr. Bennett and another man he could only assume was Mr. Cain chuckled and elbowed one another. The smell of cigars and exhaust blanketed the air.

The announcer came back. "You may pre-stage at this time."

The two cars made their way down the lanes, stopping just before the starting line. The drivers got out, leaving the doors open for their racers to enter in their place. Deidra and the large man she referred to as Robert got into their seats and slammed their doors behind them.

"Good evening," the announcer began. "Tonight we present two gems from the past, suped up and rebuilt for your viewing pleasure." The announcer addressed the stands filled with over 300 drunken spectators.

Applause broke out and then was silenced as the voice came through the speakers again. "Our reigning champion will be driving a 1933 Rolls Royce Phantom II. It has been revived from the dead, tricked out and painted dark purple. This Rolls pre-dates World War II and was the last release of the six-cylinder cars inspired by Fredrick Henry Royce himself. Performance is enhanced at higher speeds due to its lightweight design. Since there weren't many of these beauties made to begin with, this car is truly spectacular!"

Deidra waved to the crowd in the stands and then rolled up her window as the announcer patiently waited for them to settle down their excitement.

"In the left lane, we have a 1947 Buick from the Super 50 series! What a spacious ride! This heavy sedan has been painted in a classic glossy black and its chrome restored. There is a lot of power in that 8-cylinder engine!"

The PA speakers crackled as the announcer paused long enough for cheers from the stands. "Our starter may now approach the lanes," the voice said.

A woman with a crop of fiery red hair, cut into a short bob, stepped down from the stands. The sounds of whistles and howls took over. She was squeezed into a tight white dress that clung to her body like cellophane. Her body appeared to struggle as her outfit and heels only permitted tiny steps. The woman carried with her a small white scarf to serve as a flag.

Deidra glanced over at Robert, expecting to see him panic stricken and his eyes glued to the track before them. Instead, she was taken aback as he was staring straight back into her face in return. He was directing thoughts of intimidation mojo and mental voodoo at her. *He's just trying to psych me out*, she thought, turning her attention back to the redhead standing in front of them.

The woman in the white dress motioned for Deidra and Robert to pull forward and roll into the staged position. When they were in the right place, she put her hand out flat, signaling for them to stop. They were ready to go.

The woman nodded to each of them before taking a few steps backward, making sure to place herself perfectly between the two racers' cars. As she raised the flag into the air above her smoldering mane, the audience hushed instantly. Robert and Deidra both revved their engines in anticipation of the flag's let down.

Deidra sucked in a deep breath and then timed the slow exhale to match the motion of the flag. The woman brought the flag down with full force and the two cars rushed past her in a harmonic blaze that shook most of the crowd out of their seats and into standing position.

Deidra shifted gears as fast as she could only to see Robert's Buick fly past her. She cringed as his Super began to run into part of her lane just ahead of her. "Get out of the way!" she yelled through the windshield.

Robert broke past the finish line. Deidra sailed through just behind him and slammed her fist down on the dash in defeat. She allowed her foot to press the brake gently so that she could glide to a stop. *He took up my lane!* She had every intention of complaining to an official as soon as they returned to the pit area.

As she steadied her car, something caught her attention from the corner of her eye. She looked over to the left to see the Buick just before it lost control and went skidding toward a group of trees. Two men positioned at the end of the track ran toward the Buick. The car slammed into a thick tree. She could hear the car's body crumple and the sounds of glass shatter upon impact. She clutched her steering wheel and quickly turned the Rolls toward the wreck.

She stopped her car at a short distance behind the Buick, waiting for Robert to pull himself out and laugh at her for losing, but he didn't. A cloud of thick dirt enveloped his car. The two men were now close to the accident and one of them began to take pictures while the other pulled out a tiny digital recorder. She turned her car off and opened the door. Afraid to step out, she leaned the top of her body through the doorframe and looked behind her to the stands. She could see a wave of people running toward them. The cloud of dirt thinned out and she could see that there was no movement from inside the Buick.

Deidra couldn't leave Robert alone inside the mangled car. She wanted to let him know that people were coming to help. She moved toward him, expecting to see blood, knowing that he would be a mess. She then motioned for the two men with the camera and recorder to step further back. They obliged. As the man with the camera stepped back, he took photos of the air surrounding them and the wreck.

She stood next to the Buick and listened. She moved in closer even though the fumes of gasoline begged her not to. *He's fine.* She looked into the bloodied windshield and saw him slumped over, his face resting on the dash. "Robert?" she said to him softly.

The crowd of men that poured out from the stands had finally reached them. A member of Robert's team came up behind Deidra and placed his hand on her shoulder.

"Come on," he said gently. "We'll take care of him."

Deidra could see within the pile of metal and glass, a hand reaching out. She burst into tears as she lunged for it, needing to hold it in her own hands. *It's still warm!* She thought to herself. She gripped Robert's hand and felt through it. It was absent of life and meaningless. It was only flesh.

Deidra fell to her knees as members of her team surrounded her. One of them lifted her to her feet and whispered words to her in Spanish, attempting to comfort her. She removed herself from the wreckage and leaned against her car. The man with the recorder now pushed in closer, mumbling things to himself. The voices around her stung. "He's dead. My God," they confirmed. "Did the photographer get anything?"

Edward approached her cautiously. Deidra looked up and wiped away her tears. But then something changed within her. The sheer cruelty of competition provoked her mind and polluted her soul again.

"Who won?" she had to know.

Edward, thrown off-guard by the callousness of the question, opened his mouth in reaction with gaping horror. "A man is dead!" he reminded her.

"Who won?" she asked frantically.

Edward stood motionless, his eyes bulging. Deidra could see Mr. Bennett walking alongside Franklin and Mr. Cain, slowly making their way toward the accident. Without hesitation, she ran up to them, stopping abruptly before them and flashing a wild look of anticipation. She interrupted their conversation but didn't care. She had to know.

"Well?" she asked with force. "Who won?"

"... and was the photographer close enough? We need more of them if we are going to get anything out of this! Deidra should have taken care of that." Franklin was complaining to Mr. Bennett and anyone else that would listen, ignoring Deidra.

"Who won?" She stood directly in front of Franklin and looked desperately into his eyes.

Franklin looked at Mr. Bennett and swallowed before answering her. "Robert won."

Deidra pulled the wig from her head, causing an explosion of hairpins to fall to the ground. As they scattered about her feet, her arms went limp and she dropped the wig and began to shake. "How can he be the winner?" her words quivered and her lips trembled.

Franklin stepped in closer. "Robert finished first," his tone was harsh.

"No," Deidra protested. "He was in my lane!" she yelled, causing people to turn in her direction.

"This isn't the time," Franklin scolded her.

"What did the official say?" Deidra demanded.

Mr. Bennett stepped forward and frowned. "He said Robert won."

Deidra put her hands to her face and closed her eyes in disbelief. "I'm so sorry, Collin," she offered, feeling both sympathy and guilt.

Mr. Bennett put on a broad smile. "We had to lose sometime, my dear," his face was soft and the way he spoke made Deidra feel like her boss had more sympathy for her loss than for Mr. Cain's. "It's just a race."

"It's anything *but* a race ..." Deidra looked at Mr. Bennett's hand and saw the envelope. Its pale brown color and threatening reputation gave her a chill.

Franklin moved Deidra aside and clapped his hands together as a means to gain attention. "There will be no ceremony tonight," he began. He waited a moment for the curious on-lookers to turn themselves away from the separation of Robert's body from his car. When he had their interest, Franklin continued. "Due to tonight's tragedy, we will be leaving the premises early so that a cleanup can be completed thoroughly and in a timely manner. Please return to your vehicles for an immediate evacuation. Thank you."

Franklin turned to Mr. Cain and shook his hand. It was in an offer of congratulations but, at the same time, an offer of condolence for his loss. He then parted from the group quickly. There were details of the cleanup to attend to.

Deidra watched as Franklin gave out instructions to members of each racing team. The men moved quickly to gather pieces of the wreckage and place them neatly into a pile. A flatbed truck was on its way to take what was left of the Buick and Franklin had an 18-wheeler on call specifically for dealing with the unpredictableness of drag racing. A black helicopter swooped down and flew close overhead, hovering above them like a menacing metal cloud. Franklin waved at it and opened his cell phone, "It's okay," he assured its passengers.

In the noise and wind of the helicopter, Deidra's hair thrashed her face. She stood, without reaction, glaring at the back of Franklin's head. She threw down the keys to the Rolls Royce and stomped away from the chaos, heading back toward her sedan.

Edward followed her with his eyes and then turned to look at Mr. Bennett as he folded the large brown envelope and placed it inside his jacket. Mr. Bennett caught his stare and smiled weakly in return. The helicopter pulled away and dematerialized into the night. It returned into non-existence. There were no lights to trace its path.

Deidra's walk was fast-paced and fueled with anger. She had already reached the finish line of the track by the time Edward noticed.

Myrna Loy. That was her name. Edward ran the length of the coast down area. "Deidra!" he called.

"Leave me alone!" she demanded.

"Wait," he reached her and slowed himself to a speed walk alongside her, his chest heaving. "Are you all right?"

"Why shouldn't I be?" she answered sharply. "I guess you won't have to worry about me giving in to Franklin tonight. He hasn't even looked at me once!"

Edward swung her around by the arm to stop her from getting away. She pulled her arm away from him hard and glared at him. Edward was past his boiling point with her dramatics. "What is wrong with you?" he yelled. "You tell me what a jerk he's been to you and then you ask me to keep you from going home with him! Now you want his attention? A man died tonight in a race you were a part of! Don't you care about anything besides yourself?"

Deidra looked past him for a second and then back at his face. "I try not to let death affect me the way it does other people," she stated dryly. "And I care about it more than you know."

Edward studied her. She had seen so much in her life. She had grown accustomed to lying and cheating the system as those within the system allowed her to do it. She surrounded herself with high society gangsters that applauded the fact that she was risking her life to bring more profit to their gambling operation. Edward couldn't blame her for becoming insensitive. Mortality was part of a game to her now.

"I'm going home," she said peacefully and turned to finish stomping toward her car. Edward stood alone, trying to imagine her pain. He could hear the sound of footsteps behind him. Edward turned slowly and greeted Franklin with a plastic smile.

"She can be difficult," Franklin grumbled.

"Deidra?" Edward played off his interest. "I try not to get involved with her personal life ..."

"I know you spend time with her," Franklin said. "Does she talk about me?" Edward could feel his heart pushing against him. "No," he answered, but his lack of eye contact confessed otherwise.

Franklin looked behind him and sighed. "It can be too much at times," he said before facing Edward again. "She needs a good friend to help her through it. I can't be there for her as much as she wants me to be."

Edward watched as a group of men worked in unison to lift the crumpled Buick onto the flatbed parked beside them.

"I deal with more than she wants to believe. I am stretched between many people and I have obligations to all of them. She deserves more than I can give her," he admitted with grace.

"I don't understand," Edward said in attempt to buy more time. He was uncomfortable standing face to face with Franklin as he disclosed what he was afraid would become the detailed eccentricities of his relationship with the woman he was falling for.

"I know you want her," Franklin said. "It's not hard to see that."

Edward bit his lip and shifted his eyes nervously. "She's not my type," he lied. Mendacity.

Franklin let out a hearty laugh. "I'm not upset about it. I knew from the first day I met you. Honestly, Eddie. When she brought you in, I could have killed you for witnessing too much. I could have also killed you for trying to take Deidra from me, but did I?" he asked. "No. I couldn't."

Edward's discomfort increased. He had mixed feelings of confusion and doubt. He was reluctant to say anything, but had to do something besides standing there feeling trapped by Franklin's stare. He wished he could hate her. He wanted to prove that a woman could not own him, but she did.

"Well, you have nothing to worry about. She doesn't like me very much," Edward responded.

"That's because she doesn't know you yet. You don't give yourself enough credit ..."

The last thing Edward needed was a pep talk. "I don't have anything. She's used to being wined and dined ... taking private jets at the blink of an eye. I'm just a guy. I have debt and bills. I have to set money aside for my mother. Deidra ... or whatever woman comes along ... doesn't want a man like me," his frustration spilled out. Franklin obviously knew how he felt about her, so why should he hide it? He didn't have anyone to talk to about it anyway. Pent up inside, it was bound to consume him. "Not that I'm interested in her. Because I'm totally not."

Franklin placed a hand on Edward's elbow and squeezed with affection. "Your mother has already been taken care of. Stop sending her money. It's time for you to focus on yourself."

"What do you mean?" his heart skipped. Scenarios, filled with all kinds of horror, raced through his mind.

"Think, Eddie," Franklin urged. "No matter how bad it got, did you ever really need anything? When she moved from job to job, were you two ever really struggling to get by?"

Edward's brain ached. Someplace inside, he was preparing himself for the bombshell Franklin was about to deliver. A tingling sensation invaded his brain, and then numbness. He felt light-headed and took a few steps back.

"I put you through college. I made sure that you would always be taken care of," Franklin paused to allow Edward to remember to breathe.

Edward couldn't find the words to express his anger. "What?" He worked hard to keep from fainting. He prayed to all things holy that his conversation was not about to turn into a revelation reminiscent of Darth Vader's to Luke Skywalker.

"I knew your father," Franklin began. Edward was relieved but didn't feel that he was out of the clear yet and waited to hear more.

"We were fraternity brothers. He started dating your mother when we were 19," Franklin's recalled as his brow grew heavy and creased in deep thought. "He wasn't good enough for her. He tried to make their relationship look trivial. When he would bring her to parties, he would flirt with other girls in front of her. My God, Eddie. Your mother was beautiful. I could tell that she adored him, but he was cold. He ignored her."

"Then one day he left her for a girl that he later married. The day after he broke up with your mother, she came to the fraternity house looking for him. I let her in and she cried in my arms. She told me that she was pregnant."

Edward felt a hole piercing his stomach. He never knew who his father was, nor did he care. Franklin's face filled with emotion when he spoke of Edward's mother and it made him feel ill.

"I was heartbroken for her. She didn't have much and now she was going to raise a child alone. There is nothing more damaging than being alone," Franklin continued. "I knew your mother from high school. She wasn't the type of girl my parents would have allowed me to date, but I disobeyed them and took her to the prom against their wishes."

The man in the velvet suit.

"I never touched your mother or disrespected her in any way. When I saw her with that ... your father, I was appalled. I loved her. She was sacred to me, like the Madonna. I offered to marry her when she was three months along with you, but she turned me down. She knew my parents would disown me and she didn't want me to raise a child that was not mine."

Edward was fuming inside. He could feel the tears forming in his eyes and held on to them as hard as he could. Franklin grabbed Edward and embraced him like a son, but Edward was a rag doll in his arms.

"I've kept tabs on you for years. I have your eighth grade picture in my wallet. I wanted to tell you everything when I first saw you, but I couldn't."

Edward backed away from him and brushed off his sleeves. "You got me that office and that car didn't you?" he asked.

"I provided the means for it to happen, yes."

"Well, thanks for accomplishing everything for me."

"Eddie," Franklin reached for him.

"No! This is creepy," he protested adamantly. "I want to talk to my mother and I just want you to leave me alone, okay?" Edward pointed a finger at him and backed further away in discomfort.

"Eddie, I told her not to tell you. I had the money placed into her account each month. And I wouldn't discuss anything with your mother until you've calmed down. She doesn't know anything about me anymore. This life," he twirled around with his arms outward to acknowledge the activity around them, "isn't hers."

Edward sneered at him. "This is psychotic."

"You can't tell her about any of this, Eddie," Franklin's voice deepened. "As much as I love her, I won't hesitate to kill her if you do."

15

Edward drove in a blur back to Mike's apartment. He knew he wouldn't sleep that night. He wondered how he was supposed to feel. He spent hours thinking about it. He was tempted to text Deidra to ask if she knew about the situation with his mother, but couldn't find the strength to. Thoughts of Franklin lusting over his mother terrorized him throughout the night and early morning. It sickened him to think that a criminal had put him through school. If Franklin was telling the truth, then he had been raised by filthy money and, worse, with his mother's consent.

Edward sat awake on the living room couch, zoning out on TV infomercials. He was sure that Mike was still asleep and wondered what time he would wake up. Edward was hungry and wanted to ask Mike if he would be interested in a taco run.

His phone rang and he jumped with a start. He grabbed it from the end table next to him. "Hello?" he said after taking a moment to catch his breath. He glanced at the clock sitting on the bar that separated the kitchen from the living room. It was 7 a.m.

"Hi." It was Deidra.

"Jesus," Edward whispered. "I thought you were my mother. What are you doing up?"

"I wanted to apologize for the way I acted last night. You were right. I was being selfish," she said.

"It's all right."

"What did Franklin want?" she asked.

"What do you mean?" he asked in return defensively.

"I saw him walking up when we were talking. That's why I left so quickly," she replied.

"Oh." Edward could see the replay of her walking away from him again in his mind. "Yeah, he didn't really say much."

Deidra sat in silence, waiting for Edward to continue speaking, but he didn't. "You didn't talk about me?"

"No," Edward lied.

Deidra giggled and then clicked her tongue. "There I go again thinking everything's about me," she joked.

Edward could hear Mike moving around in his room. His bedroom door opened and he staggered across the hall and into the bathroom.

"Hold on, Deidra," Edward said before pulling the phone away from his face to yell at Mike, "Hey, you want some tacos?"

Mike said something that was too muffled to understand and Edward could hear the sound of urine splashing into the toilet.

"I have to go," Edward told her, feeling the pangs of hunger taunting him.

"Okay," she said.

"Are you doing anything tonight?" he asked.

"Well, yes," she sounded hesitant to answer.

"Please don't tell me it's with *him*," he begged.

"No," Deidra began. "It's with Collin ... Mr. Bennett. He's taking me to dinner to try and make me feel better about what happened."

"Oh, that's nice of him. On a Saturday?" he asked.

"I know. He's like that though. He doesn't care what people think. We go to lunch sometimes and people look at me like I am his mistress. His wife knows me. She's really nice," she stopped for a moment. "I asked him if we could just have dinner at his place so I could visit with her, too, but he said she wasn't feeling well."

"Well, I'm not doing anything," Edward informed her. "Maybe Mike will want to get some beers."

"I'll talk to you later," she said. "Okay, bye."

Mike lumbered out from the bathroom. His arms hung like dead branches and his face was bloated. He acknowledged Edward with a grunt as he opened a kitchen cabinet door, revealing a colorful assortment of coffee mugs. "I hate instant coffee."

"I asked you if you wanted some tacos. I'm sure they have coffee there," Edward replied.

"I'm too tired to drive," Mike whined. "I have to have a cup of coffee before I can do anything. I have to have a coffee just to go get another coffee ... or tacos."

"I'll get them," Edward offered.

"But you can't drive standard."

"I have a car."

Mike looked at him with one raised eyebrow. "What?"

"I have a car," Edward repeated.

"Where?"

"Outside."

"How did you get it?"

Edward knew that no matter how he broke the news to Mike, he wouldn't understand. "Mr. Bennett gave me a bonus," he tried to say it like it was the truth. Like it was really possible that the new guy could get a Mercedes as a bonus. After a month on the job.

Mike laughed and then looked at Edward. "Are you serious?" he asked.

"Yes."

"For doing what?" Mike's tone bordered on disbelief and hatred.

"I helped get some big accounts."

Mike slammed his coffee mug on the countertop, silencing Edward. He exited the kitchen to step closer toward Edward and glared at him. "What kind of car?" he asked hoping it would be a beat-down green pinto.

Edward looked at the TV. It was trying to sell him a bathroom cleaner that would clean tile grout without scrubbing. He now wished he had gone to his mother's for the weekend. "A Mercedes ..."

"A WHAT?" Mike yelled with his arms in front of him. "How the hell ...? I have done nothing but kiss Mr. Bennett's ass for three years!"

"Mike ..."

"I get you a job and within a *month* you get a huge office, a nice car, and now you're doing Deidra!"

Edward rolled his eyes and slumped back into the couch.

"What the fuck kind of shit is that?" Mike asked.

Edward shrugged his shoulders.

"I work. I do a job. I have accounts and proven profit records."

"I work, too."

"Really, Eddie? Do you?"

Edward calmly got up from the couch and grabbed his cell phone and new car keys from the table next him. He walked toward the door without so much as a glance at Mike.

"Where are you going?" Mike called to him, still hardened with anger.

"I'm going to get some tacos," Edward answered simply. "Happy fuckin' Saturday!"

இ௸ஓ

Edward hit a drive-thru and sat inside his car and ate. He was parked just outside the quasi-Mexican restaurant that provided him with a greasy taco breakfast. He could feel the eyes of patrons staring at him from their tables inside. Edward didn't want to be around anyone.

After making a decision against eating a third taco, he decided to stay at a motel for the evening. It was only mid-morning, but he wanted to get the room as soon as he could and get some much needed sleep. He wanted to buy a bottle of rum as well. Thoughts of Franklin and the night before were hanging over him.

Edward looked into the restaurant, focusing on a small child stuffing his pudgy face with ground beef and sour cream until something caught his attention moving a few yards away from his car. A man dressed in tattered jeans and a discolored shirt that obviously used to be white, was holding out his hand to every person passing by.

He had stationed himself near the sidewalk at an intersection, hoping to collect as much charity as he could. His shoes were loose and his hair graying.

Edward put the fresh taco back into the paper bag and exited his car. He approached the man with care, not wanting to startle him. Edward cleared his throat to warn of his arrival. "Excuse me, sir?"

The man swung around and smiled. He could see the food in Edward's hand. "Yes?"

"You can have this," Edward offered. The man reached forward and accepted the taco happily. "You are a very kind young man!" he praised.

"Thank you," Edward said as he turned to walk away.

"Young man?" the old man called. "I cannot accept such a beautiful meal without giving you something in return," the man announced in a formal tone.

Edward tensed a little. "I don't want anything for it," he explained.

The man walked up to Edward and stood directly before him. Edward could see the gloss of perspiration on his face and inhaled the body odor surrounding him. He did his best to look unaffected by how strong the smell was.

"Let me tell you a story," the man insisted.

"No," Edward tried. "I should be going ..."

"It won't be that bad," the man tried to assure him. "You might like it."

Edward, as sorry as he felt for the man, wanted nothing to do with the awkward story time. He was sleep deprived and desperate to get into a bed. Sleeping on the floor at Mike's had worn thin. The last few nights he tried stuffing himself into various positions on the sofa but ended up paying for it in neck cramps that only grew progressively worse throughout the day. He was now glad that Mike blew up at him. Edward needed an excuse to get out of that tiny apartment.

"There was once a prince who lived alone in a dark, empty castle," the old man began. Edward could see a twinkle in his eye. He was certain the man had children at one point. Telling stories was how he reconnected with better times.

"The prince had nothing but his big castle and tons of gold. One day, a bird flew into the castle and told the young prince that a beautiful princess was traveling in their direction."

Edward opened his eyes wider, humoring the old man. *Great.* He hoped the story would end quickly so he could find a decent motel room, take a shower, turn off his cell phone, and get some rest.

The old man eyed his taco with delight. "I sure am hungry! Would you like to sit with me while I eat? I can tell you the rest of the story when I am done."

"No, that's all right. Go ahead and eat. I should be going," Edward reminded the man.

"Okay, young man! I'll finish the story first. I want you to hear it. A story for a taco!" The old man's face was brown from the sun's rays and years of hardship.

Edward relaxed his posture and remembered that he had no place to go. He stepped toward a hedge that was a part of the landscaping job on the restaurant's property so that he was out of the way of cars going to the drive-thru window. He searched himself for enthusiasm. "I'm listening."

"The prince prepared his castle. He cleaned it from top to bottom! And just like the bird told him, a princess did arrive. She had dinner with the prince. After they ate and talked, the prince realized that he was very attracted to her."

Edward nodded to let the man know that he was paying attention.

"The princess told the prince that she had been banished from her kingdom by her own father. The king had always kept his distance from her when she was a child. She never felt loved by him. When he told her to leave town and never come back, she asked him why. The king told her that she was cursed. That some years before, her father made a wizard angry. The wizard told the king that his only daughter would never have a prince because her tongue was poison."

Edward watched as the man swayed to the rhythm of his own words.

"The prince didn't believe in curses. And to prove it, he told the princess that he would marry her if she would have him. She liked the prince, too, but she was afraid of the curse. She didn't want to hurt him."

"The princess stayed with the prince at his castle for weeks. The prince fell in love with her and couldn't wait any longer. One night while she was sleeping, the prince went into her room and woke the princess from a deep sleep to profess his love to her. He didn't care about the curse. He wanted to kiss her. He begged her to kiss him and the princess gave in."

The man ended the telling of his passionate story and brought the taco up to his face, breathing in the warmth of it. He grinned at Edward and licked his dry, cracked lips. "Thank you for the taco."

Edward stood and watched as the man turned his full attention on the taco and left him. The man sat himself on the edge of the sidewalk facing the busy street and placed the meaty taco onto his lap. He began to unwrap it as if it were a precious jewel when Edward walked up behind him.

"Excuse me, sir?" Edward asked. "What happened to the prince?"

The man looked behind himself and then back into the street of cars swishing past before them. "What do you want to happen to him?" He then took a strong bite into the crispy corn tortilla shell.

Edward drove into the parking lot of a motel on the side of the highway. After he parked, he decided to check his bank account from his cell phone. With everything that went on the day before, he forgot to check and see how much his paycheck had been. It would have been a direct deposit at midnight on Thursday and now he needed to be sure that nothing had gone wrong with it.

He typed in his login ID and password on the phone and waited. He then validated a second security step and waited again. He didn't want to put the expense of the motel room on a credit card.

The screen showed him his account balance. It read $53,115.73.

His hand went numb. He opened his mouth in disbelief. There had to be a mistake. The last time he checked his balance he had about $3,400 in his account and only expected to be paid just under a couple thousand that pay period. In a normal world, it would not have made any sense to him. But his world stopped being normal about a month ago.

He closed the browser. His first instinct was to inform the bank that they had made a mistake, but after thinking for a moment, he knew better. The money had been placed into his account intentionally. They were paying him for his soul and attempting to comfort him for the loss of his ethics and morals. He would now be expected to go along with anything and everything.

Edward sat, contemplating the situation. He could complain to Franklin and refuse the money so he could feel good about himself. That would only endanger his life and possibly his mother's. Or he could play the game for what it was worth and start living in ways he had only dreamed of. *What if the money keeps coming in?* He could start putting a large portion of it away and never have to worry about retirement.

It was too much to think about. His mind needed rest. Moral dilemmas would have to wait. Edward looked up at the motel's neon lights, advertising its vacancy. He scanned the perimeter. It was depressing and lined with filth. He started his car and headed for the access road. He remembered seeing a group of massive, upscale hotels in the center of the downtown area and they had suddenly become his style.

16

His cell phone rang. Edward peeked at the digital display of a clock on the nightstand next to him. It was 8:32 p.m. He had spent most of Saturday in a deep sleep.

He pulled the phone from his pants pocket and answered it. "Hello?"

"Where are you?" Deidra asked.

"In a hotel."

"Why?"

"Mike's pissed off at me. I don't know. What's going on? Did you call over there?" he asked.

"I went over. Mike said he didn't know where you were. He was kinda rude."

"I'm moving out soon anyway, I guess." Edward yawned.

She paused hesitantly. "Can I come over?"

He waited for room service with a glass of wine in his hand. He ordered an assortment of appetizers in haste, asking for suggestions from the man taking his order on the phone.

She arrived at the same time as the food. She poured herself a glass of wine while Edward signed for the food and tip. She sipped her cabernet and waited as Edward lifted a shiny, silver-colored lid and took in the aroma.

Edward picked up a plate and served himself some baked ravioli before taking a seat on the end of the bed. Deidra sat on a chair next to a desk across from him and smiled. "Hungry?"

"Sorry, I've been sleeping all day. Would you like some?"

She shook her head. "No. I had dinner with Mr. Bennett an hour ago, remember?"

Edward removed a piece of ravioli from his lips to answer. "Oh! Right! I forgot."

"I wish I could forget," she said as she looked down into her glass of wine.

Edward sat his plate aside on the bed and leaned forward with concern. "What happened?"

Deidra took a sip of wine and then bit down on the edge of her lip, thinking of how to begin. She didn't like to tell him too much or too little. The balance in between was hard for her to gauge.

"Mr. Bennett called me last night on my cell while I was driving home from the track," she began. "You know ... from the race. He told me to meet him at a seafood place we sometimes go to for dinner on Saturday night. You know ... today. Anyway, when I got there, he had a private room reserved in the back. I didn't think anything of it at first, but as soon as I was escorted in there and saw him, I figured out why. He wanted to talk business." She paused to drink the last of her wine.

"We ordered our food and started talking. He told me that he knew I was close to Franklin and he felt comfortable enough letting me in on things because of his trust in Franklin. He said that he had been asked to do something unusual. He got some phone call that afternoon at his house and was given some instructions." She stopped and stood to collect herself and to pour another glass of wine. She took in a deep breath and tried to hold the bottle steady in her hand but it shook, spilling over onto the carpet.

Edward stood to help her clean it up. She sat back into her chair, ignoring the spill, and continued. "He asked me to kill someone."

"What?" Edward was surprised. Then he realized that he was surprised about being surprised and abandoned his cleaning effort, leaving the napkin on the floor. He stood, looking down at her and waited with anticipation for her to finish.

"He told me that it was too important to hire someone else for and that he only trusted me, Franklin, and a few other people. He looked like a wreck. Like he had been, I don't know … threatened or something. His face was … old." She looked outside the window at the man-made lights drowning out the stars in the skyline.

"Are you going to do it?" he asked excitedly, afraid of her answer.

"I can't." She was disappointed with herself. "I can't explain to you right now why, but I can't kill like that. There has to be a reason."

"Good," he sighed. He was relieved.

"No. Not good. This has something to do with that envelope. I told you something big was going to happen with this race! Remember?"

"Yeah. That stuff Franklin was upset about."

"Right! Now poor Mr. Bennett has to do something horrible and I'm too weak to help him! He trusts me. Besides, it's my fault for losing the race. I should have said yes but … he won't tell me who it is or why." Regret plagued her.

"But he can't just ask you to do something like that. You've never killed anyone before," Edward stopped in doubt. "Have you?"

She hesitated a little too long. "No. Not for him."

"Well? Then why would he expect you to now? Then what hap—wait … what?" He stopped for a moment and looked at her as she shrugged. He decided to move past it.

"He looked upset and then told me that he cared about me. He said he didn't want to have to force me to do it. So he's going to try and think of something but he doesn't have much time. He said something about it needing to be done soon."

"So, he didn't tell you who it was? The person they want dead?"

"No."

Edward grabbed the bottle of wine and topped off his glass. "That's pretty crazy."

Deidra looked around the room in sudden confusion. The room didn't suit his personality. And neither did the wine or appetizers. "What the fuck is going on with this room?"

"What do you mean?" He sipped his wine again, knowing what she meant.

She shook her head.

"Eddie, I don't know who else Mr. Bennett would ask to help him take care of this."

"What does it matter?"

"What if he asks *you*?" she posed the question in an effort to shift his thinking.

Edward thought for a moment before dismissing it completely. "He wouldn't," he stated confidently. "He doesn't know me."

"He knows that I know you. You're in the club. I'm sure he's thought of it," she pressed further.

He tightened his jaw, thinking about Mr. Bennett asking him to kill someone. It was too absurd. But to Edward, so was asking Deidra to do it. "I just don't think he will."

"If he does, I'll do it for you," Deidra volunteered with the sound of honor in her voice.

"What? Why?" he panicked for her. The fact that she kept voicing doubt about her decision to turn down Mr. Bennett's offer scared him. She was too loyal to these monsters.

"Because I want to know," she answered. "I want to know who's such a damn threat to the system that they would have to be taken out like this. I want to know who it is."

Edward's stomach turned at the thought of it. Her sense of adventure was twisted. He didn't want her to know because then he would know.

"Why would you want to get yourself any more involved with this stuff? Even if you did agree to do it, they wouldn't be stupid enough to tell you what you were really doing," he tried to sound convincing, as if his mission was to be the voice of reason, but came off sounding like a coward instead.

"Eddie, these people don't waste their time on small jobs. When we race and somebody takes the envelope—that's considered a small job. It's all part of a game. This is different. This job was handed down. This is not the kind of thing Franklin gets involved in normally." Her voice was heavy with passion. The emphasis that she placed on her words were meant to reach him, to break him from the conditioning he had endured throughout his life.

He had to look away from her. He wasn't about to let her convince him that her morbid curiosity was valid. "I don't care who it is, and I think that you should stay as far away from it as possible."

Deidra placed her empty glass on the desk and approached him. She tilted her head and tried looking up into his face, but he was keeping his distance mentally. He looked through her and onto the floor.

"These people could shut down the entire world in less than 10 minutes." She spoke with a quieted tone that chilled him. "They could start a war anytime they want to, anywhere they want to. The corporations own the media. They can make you believe anything they want. They have everything at their disposal and more. If they want someone dead, I want to know who it is."

"*They?* Who are *they?*" He used to like his reality. Deidra was warping things.

"They are the people who handed down this job to Franklin and then to Mr. Bennett. They are the ones running things. Everything."

"Why do you want to know who they are after?" he asked sharply.

"Because I just do."

Edward sat on the edge of the bed and placed his head into his hands. Frustration overwhelmed him. "Wouldn't you be happy with a normal life? Haven't you ever thought about getting married, having kids and stuff like that?"

"Yes. But I know not to. I don't want to care about things like that. Caring about people makes you weak."

"You don't care about anyone?" he asked.

"Not in the ways society thinks I should." She was preoccupied. "I'm going to call Mr. Bennett and tell him I'll do it," she added quickly.

"No!"

Deidra pointed a finger at him and put on a menacing tone. "Don't talk to anyone about this. And I don't want you trying to stop me!"

They both jumped as the sound of Edward's phone cut through. Deidra placed a hand to her chest and laughed while trying to catch her breath.

Edward reached for the phone and looked at the numbers on its screen. "It's Mike."

He answered after taking a second to collect his thoughts. "Hello?"

"Edward, it's Mike," Mike said sternly.

"I know."

"I want you to come and get all your shit out of my apartment. Tonight."

Edward was stunned in reaction to Mike's callousness. "What? Come on, man. I don't even have a place yet ..."

"You've had enough time! I'm sure you can afford it. And if you can't, you can sleep in your new car! Leave your key under the doormat."

And with that, Mike ended the call.

Edward threw his phone across the room, hitting the bathroom door. He looked over to Deidra and wished that she had a softer personality. Just once he wanted to see her let down her guard and act more … *God. Am I a chauvinist?*

"What happened?" she asked.

"Mike kicked me out."

17

It was late. Jake couldn't sleep because that kind of thing just didn't happen for him anymore. Every shot of tequila he forced himself to take should have helped, but it didn't. *I'm safe,* he had to convince himself every night. There just could not be another night like that one in August.

His feet felt cold against the sheets in his bed. It was the same pleasant chill he got from the sheets in those hotel beds. Freshly laundered, but washed so many times that he still wondered too many things about their hygiene. He spent many nights in hotels now.

Check the curtains, study the shadows, turn on the closet light...

That one night was the only time he had screamed in such terror. That one night was real and it haunted his memories. The visuals of it were burned into his mind. He remembered being able to taste his own death coming and only wished that it would quicken. The way that night's terror replayed, he knew it was forever.

Dr. Hammond, as he most preferred to be called, was not a tall man, a short man, or anything but average in height. He usually wore an interesting beard that came out red in color with a few gray specks, but recently styled it into a goatee. His face was fair and filled with freckles. He had lines about his eyes and mouth from the days when he used to smile and spend time in the sun on his motorcycle, and the red hair atop his head had thinned out. He was the type of professor that liked to wear suspenders to mark his eccentricities and to relax his students' perception of him. He hated bow ties and striped socks. He loved a bagel with cream cheese and a coffee every morning.

He was not into sports. The only sport he used to tolerate was European football. But he had changed so much in the last few years that many of his interests had faded. He was now an alcoholic obsessed with UFO websites and alien studies.

He vowed to be more prepared when they returned. He knew they would. There was a plan in his head. He rehearsed his speech each night before sleep finally came. His nightly ramblings only changed when he imagined a new set of questions for them. He wasn't going to be caught off guard this time. And any night could be the one, so he had to be ready. It had to be perfect.

He laughed to himself at the sight of the nightlight he had plugged into the wall beside him. *Jesus, it's like I'm trying to see them.*

The abduction story was something he had learned to hide. It had already caused a divorce and a narrowing in the number of friends he once kept. It would devastate him if it was leaked on campus. He wondered sometimes if it had been and if they made fun of him at frat parties. But as far as he knew, it was still his secret.

He started the countdown in his mind to induce sleep. It was self-hypnosis he had learned on the Internet. Herbal sleep supplements and chamomile tea also seemed to help. He was almost there, close to sleep, when the lights began to flicker like they did on August 11th.

"Oh my God!"

Jake shot up in his bed and ran toward the window. As he pulled the cord on those cheap mini blinds he had always been meaning to replace, a bright light flooded the room. He had to shield his face as he stepped backward, panic stricken at the thought of reliving the nightmare he had endured once before.

He threw himself back into bed and pulled the comforter over his head. He folded into the fetal position and tightened his eyes shut as hard as he could. A vibrating hum filled the air around the room for only seconds. Then it was silent. Something cleared its throat to break the tension.

"Um, excuse me," it said in a human voice.

Jake summoned the strength to slowly remove the blanket from his head and peek out. They were exactly as he remembered. The two of them stood, naked, pale, and only about three feet tall. Their large black eyes a hideous sight, as they had tormented him in his nightmares.

"I have waited a long time to ask you some questions," Jake Hammond began bravely. "Would that be acceptable to you? For me … to ask, I mean?"

The aliens standing before him at the side of his bed looked at one another as Jake continued.

"Why did you choose me?" he asked, petrified with fear.

"There is no plan in choosing anyone. Sorry to disappoint you." One of them answered without the movement of its thin lips.

"Oh," Jake answered in a trembling voice. "Are you the same ones that took me into your ship before?"

"Uh … no," the other one answered. "We work in shifts."

"Did you just speak English?" Jake gasped.

"Yeah, It's not hard to learn. You can meow like a cat, right?" The alien on the left answered as they both erupted into laughter. Their bodies jiggled and wiggled up and down as their heads bobbled like cartoon characters. The sound that came from their tiny mouths was similar to a small child's giggle.

"What is your interest in my planet?" Jake continued, confused by their humor.

"Oh shit. We made a wrong turn!" the one on the right said playfully. "Are we on planet Jake?"

They bobbed in delight together as Jake frowned. "Wait, I guess I should have asked something else … oh my God. I'm sorry. I feel so stupid."

"ANNOYING EARTH MAN!" one of them stood more erect as the other instantly bent over in hysterics. "We have business here. All of these questions ... it would be like if I showed up at your cubicle and started asking a bunch of stupid shit about where you purchased your shoes."

The other alien laughed so hard it began to let out a tiny snorting sound.

"Yeah," the alien tried hard not to smile and discreetly kicked at its partner that was doubled over on the floor. "So let us get back to what we are doing."

"What are you doing?" Jake asked.

The alien on the floor composed itself and sighed. "We are trying to give you an implant."

"What?!"

The alien standing then bent over to hit the other one on the arm. "Hey! You're supposed to let me strap them down before saying that!"

Jake squirmed under his covers. "What purpose does the implant serve?"

"Dude, it's so way beyond you to know that right now," the one on the floor explained sarcastically. "But remember this, human. You need to go to Las Vegas soon. That's where Dr. Fitzpatrick will take out the implant. The fate of your planet depends on you."

"Don't tell him that."

"Why not?"

"Fate of the planet?"

"Technically, yes ..."

"Look, you're just supposed to tell him to go see Fitzpatrick. Don't mess him all up with some fate-of-the-planet talk," the other one explained. "You're putting too much pressure on his monkey-brain."

Jake developed a sudden eye-twitch and did his best to control his unsteady breathing. They were jerks, but they still frightened him. He wondered why he didn't remember any of this type of crude behavior happening before.

"The human just called you fat. Did you hear that?"

"We can hear your thoughts, you know."

"He thinks you are fat and I am sexy."

"I ... I ... I didn't think anything!" Jake protested. "I just want you to leave ... please."

"So, I'm not sexy?"

"Look," Jake cleared his throat. "Last time it wasn't like this. It was serious and the other guys were not laughing at me or making fun of me. It was less humiliating."

"Well, that was bullshit. No more fake memories for you, human."

"Now you know the drill," the other one chimed in. "Time to pull your trousers down!"

"Pants. They call them pants now."

"Pants. Pull them down."

"What? Why?" Jake pleaded.

"Just kidding!" they laughed. "Just gimmie your arm so I can put this in. Then you can go back to bed and cry."

Jake froze. His body was numb and his head was light. He held his right arm out involuntarily and watched as they used what could be best compared to a stapler to insert the implant. He couldn't speak. Within seconds it was over.

"Ok, now although this will prevent pregnancy, you should still use protection for a few weeks just in case ..."

"Stop it!" the other alien said during a fit of laughter that caused tears to well up in his large eyes. "You are so damn funny!"

"Okay, Human. It is time for us to leave you."

"Stop making me laugh!" the other one said.

"We love you."

"Let's check his fridge for cupcakes."

Jake lost consciousness to the sound of aliens rummaging through his kitchen.

18

Mike leaned against the wall in the hallway and glared at Edward as he dumped his dirty clothes from a laundry basket into a large brown box. Edward pushed down on the heap of wrinkled clothes to make room for more. The small amount of food he had purchased and stocked in Mike's pantry would fit on top if he could smash his clothes down enough. He swung cabinet doors open, stacking boxes of preservative-laden goods into his arms and taking them over to the large box. He hovered over the box with his stack of food, trying to figure out the best way to pack them, but soon gave up and let his arms drop, allowing the food to fall in.

He turned to Mike and sighed before speaking robotically. "All I can take right now are these boxes. The furniture and larger things won't fit in my car."

Edward had lugged a dresser, end table, weight set, an assortment of lamps, a computer, and other pieces of bachelor possessions over from Austin. Mike allowed him to stuff as many of his things as possible into an outside storage closet on the patio. The only special request Edward had made in the deal was that his computer be stored inside due to humidity. For the past month, it sat tucked away in a corner of Mike's bedroom.

"You can send for the rest of it, but I want to be here when they come and get the stuff. I want my key back now," Mike replied.

Edward shook his head in disappointment. "What the hell did I do to you, Mike?"

Deidra walked in through the open front door. "What else will fit in my car?"

He took a quick glance around the room and kicked the large box in front of him. "This is really all there is. I can put this in my car."

Mike held out his hand to Edward. "You'd better get the rest of your crap soon. I want it out of here. Send some people to get it this week ..."

"Mike! I'm not going to hire people to bring me my things! I'll call you later this week and get them myself!" Edward snapped.

"No way, man! Give me the key!" Mike yelled furiously.

Edward fumbled through his pockets trying to find his key ring. His exaggerated movements were heated by the tension he felt in the room. Deidra watched as Edward searched in vain for the key. He looked like he was about to punch holes through his pockets.

He contorted his body as if it was on fire. Deidra was amused by it until Mike caught her attention. In her peripheral view she could see Mike's limbs and facial expression. He was gloating. His arms were now crossed and his chin was lifted high. The back of his head rested on the wall behind him and on his mouth, she saw an undeniable smirk.

"I know they're here somewhere, dammit! Maybe I dropped them in this big fucking box!" Edward rummaged through the groceries and clothes, slamming the contents against the cardboard walls inside. His temper was flaring higher. "Deidra, did you see my keys outside?" he yelled.

"No," she replied calmly. She had never seen him this agitated and realized that when he was angry, he reminded her of a rabid squirrel.

Mike then stared at Deidra. He studied her face with hatred.

She acknowledged Mike with a grin. She sensed something that was faint at first, but felt it grow into something more. Clarity hit her. Mike was never this cocky. This whole thing was an act. He was in the middle of an elaborate performance. She knew this because she had seen acting at its finest often enough in her line of work. Liars, thieves, killers, business men … they all worked the same. They all put on an act in front of her.

She carefully put the pieces together and calculated the equation in her head. Then she had to force herself to look away from him.

"Here!" Edward tossed a small piece of metal at Mike, hitting the spot on the wall next to his shoulder. "Take your stupid fucking key! Come on, Deidra."

He lifted the large box and headed for the door. As Deidra followed, she turned back for a second and couldn't help but look up at Mike's face. The smirk was now a full blown smile.

∾

"What is wrong with that guy?" Edward yelled from the hotel bathroom. He splashed his face with water thinking it would help. They did it in the movies and he was confused and frustrated enough to try it. He yanked a towel off of the shelf next to him and patted his face and threw the towel down to the floor afterward. He had seen that in a movie, too.

He walked out of the bathroom and saw Deidra sitting on the bed wearing a strange look on her face. He removed his jacket and waited a minute to see if she would speak to him on her own. Her eyes raced around the room.

"What is it?" he prompted.

"Mike's the one," she answered vacantly, pulling down on the sleeve of her sweater. "He's going to do the job."

Edward stood erect and waited for it to register before responding. "There's no way."

"Why not?" she sat up straight. "It makes perfect sense. That's why he's throwing you out! That's what's going on! Think about the timing!"

She knew she was right.

Edward turned to pace the room. He thought about it as objectively as he could. "It just seems too weird. Mike isn't that type ..."

"Exactly!" she agreed with excitement.

"But why do I have to be thrown out for him to do it?"

"Because," she said with excitement, "maybe he has to use the apartment for something. Who knows? It's probably just easier that way... less to worry about. They might have told him to kick you out so you wouldn't be linked to it or something," she guessed.

"Mike's not *in* though. Also, I thought you said Mr. Bennett didn't trust many people ... that he wasn't going to hire anyone on the outside for this."

"Maybe he trusts Mike," she guessed again.

Edward couldn't picture it, but knew that in light of things, he didn't know much about anything going on in the world. Everything was a lie dressed up inside another lie. Lies got together and gave birth to more of themselves ad nauseam. And now, it seemed that Mike was going to kill someone.

"When I took some of your stuff down to my car, I made a quick call to Mr. Bennett," she confessed.

"Why?" Edward whined, throwing his hands over his head hopelessly.

"Because, Eddie. I felt bad. I wanted to help him and take the job," she explained. "But it was too late. He told me it had been taken care of." She wrung her hands in her lap.

"Damn. We should thank God you don't have to do it," he showed relief in his eyes.

Deidra looked at him in bewilderment. She didn't hear much about God anymore in a religious sense. She had been raised a Catholic, but did her best to keep it at a distance now. As an adult she made an effort to avoid any conversation that led to the actual topic of God. It had even caused some problems in her family. But she would not be a sinner and there would be no guilt felt. The Devil could not have her if she didn't believe in any of it. It had all become a strange mythology to her.

He's not really thanking God. It's just an expression, she assured herself while fidgeting her fingers. *It's not like when my brother, the saintly Father Martin, talks about God...Eddie doesn't mean it like that.*

"Well?" he asked. "Aren't you glad? I mean, I still can't see Mike doing anything like that but, whatever," he said while waving his hands in front of his face.

"I thought you two were friends?"

"We were. I guess. We were never close," Edward shook his head. "It doesn't matter."

"Well, I'm willing to bet that on Monday he won't be at work." She was sure of herself. "He'll be on this assignment. Watch." She raised her eyebrows with a look of all-knowing superiority. He couldn't possibly know how to profile his own friend the way she could.

Edward kicked off his shoes and smiled. "Good for him," he laughed. "Now he will be as screwed up as the rest of us. Maybe more. They should send Miguel with him."

"How do you know Miguel?"

"I met him a week ago. Franklin made me go with him to … It doesn't matter right now."

"Crazy Miguel?" she laughed.

"Crazy is an understatement."

Deidra gazed at Edwards shoes. "I guess I'll be going," she said while raising herself up quickly and heading for the door. "I'll see you on Monday."

"Wait," he stopped her. She froze with her arm out-stretched for the door knob and faced him. "I don't want to ask you anything about your personal life but ..."

"Then don't," she warned.

"No, it's about work," he paused to gauge her reaction and then continued. "What do you do there? Do you really work as an assistant?"

"What do you mean?" She looked at him sourly.

He shifted uncomfortably.

"I guess I mean that I usually don't see you, you know... at work. I see you bring Mr. Bennett lunch sometimes. Oh, and coffee in the morning, but," he could see the corners of her mouth begin to curve upward as he kept on. "You just seem, well, you are so smart and I guess I just don't see you as some-one's assistant."

She relaxed her posture. "Assistants do a lot. I keep Mr. Bennett together. The company wouldn't run while he's out of town or during lunch if I wasn't there. And at the same time, I am always assisting Franklin." She looked about the room, letting a fast-paced commercial catch her eye for a moment. "What do you think I would be better at?"

"I don't know," he admitted.

She turned to reach for the door again, looking back at Edward in careful thought. Her eyes turned to the ceiling and her forehead wrinkled. "I take classes. I study psychology. But the money in this business is too good."

Edward jumped forward. "You should teach someday. You need to do what feels right. Teaching could be very reward-ing. You are great at explaining things," he said, hoping to give her some encouragement.

She had a puzzled look on her face and then stared into his eyes. Sometimes she forgot how naive he was. "Maybe someday. I was thinking about teaching at the university level. I have a

Masters in art history and one in psychology. I'm working on my ..." She stopped herself.

Edward was stunned. It was a soft blow to his ego and at the same time a sobering lesson. Not only was she breath-takingly beautiful, but she was far more educated that he was. "Oh."

"I'll see you Monday." She left him standing alone in the room. He was surrounded by boxes of possessions he had once thought were valuable. Beat-up cardboard boxes had become his luggage. He imagined what the reaction would have been had he asked a bellhop to help him tote the brown eyesores up to his room. A month ago he wouldn't have cared. He now found himself struggling to resist the urge to spend his Sunday morning shopping for real luggage. Designer luggage.

I hope Mike isn't involved with these people.

19

Jake taught with a passion for history and truth. He knew from his own research that Socrates was more than a hated man. Wandering from place to place, he encountered ignorance in everyone and set out to tackle it head on. Much like a quarterback taking a charge, he took the insults and was sometimes run out of town, defeated. But there were still some that valued his lessons and stopped to ponder his seemingly ridiculous stories so that he created around himself a following of students. Jake felt just as crazy as Socrates had seemed to most people of his time.

With nothing but faith to go on, he and his students were left to sift through what Plato wrote about his Athenian teacher with a cautious eye. They were set up to believe that Socrates was nothing but a selfless man left to wander the Earth with nothing but a desire to teach some type of moral code to those he felt were otherwise lost. He was the anti-sophist, a man willing to work for free in a time when knowledge was paid for by the privileged. To instill upon humans a sense of justice that many may not have been ready to understand … it seemed imperative to the human process of evolution. But sadly, as many college students find, Socrates was not the super-human or godlike man they might have envisioned him to be before taking his course. He was instead an unattractive, poor man, treated as a public nuisance. Dr. Hammond humanized him as students learned of his nagging wife and the accusations of corruption by the very people he set out to enlighten.

So even as he sat behind the desk, staring into the image of what he was expected to swallow as being that of Socrates, the professor wondered otherwise. It was degrading to see this man's image reproduced into poster form for a profit. To make it worse, he had stabbed the poster onto the wall with cheap thumb tacks, each of them a different color. It was obscene. Having the poster properly framed had been in the back of his mind for the last year. He had certainly never intended for it to become pierced with worthless, plastic tacks at the corners. But that was how it hung.

Professor Hammond held an office on the fourth floor of the political science building on campus. His view through the only window in that office was of the parking lot below where he could look on as students parked in faculty spaces off-limits to them so that their car doors would ding his car repeatedly. It was a torture comparable to OCD. He had to look out that window every ten minutes hoping not to see it happen.

"Am I the corruptor of minds today, my friend?" He asked the Socrates on the poster. *If you only knew the horrors.*

Hammond had nothing prepared for class that day. He was supposed to re-teach the same set of notes he had used for the past five years on Nietzsche's The Antichrist. But unfortunately, he had been severely harassed by aliens a few nights earlier and had come to the stark realization that his old notes made absolutely no sense to him anymore. How could they? He was now, after all, nothing like the man he had been before.

He waited anxiously for the clock above Socrates to change. The ticking sound kept a rhythm to his shaking knees. His arm itched. Controlling the urge to scratch was easy since scratching meant that he would have to touch it. 'It' being the disgusting lump in his arm that was shaped like an ugly peanut.

This week's lesson couldn't have come with better timing. With only two days between him and the incident, having to interpret any work by Nietzsche to an auditorium of ungrateful students who only enrolled in his class to fill a political science credit requirement was brutal. The Antichrist this time around was too significant. Too ironic for him to digest completely.

The five minute marker arrived and Hammond dumped the rest of his bottled water into the potted plant on the corner of his desk. It was time to walk to class. He had to focus on his breathing, his posture, and his meditative center in order to move himself down the crowded hallways without vomiting. He was fighting off a nervous breakdown and it wouldn't become anyone else's business.

Through the door and up to the podium, Professor Hammond took his time to remember his sanity as students still trickled in from the hallways. He stared at his feet to focus on his shoelaces. *Meditate.* He stared at his fingers, hoping to make them stay still. *Remember your center.* He looked about himself for his notes only to remember again how they were on their way to the city dump. It was as if Nietzsche himself was laughing at the sick joke that had become Jake's perverted life.

They had settled in, for the most part. Students still shifted in their seats and pretended to shut off their MP3 players. They set their cell phones to vibrate so that they could still text during class. The auditorium seating took them up and above ground level and into a distance Hammond's eyes were too old now to focus on without his glasses. He was about to turn 50. He didn't feel old, but maybe worn down in some places.

It was a ritual to start the class by the staged clearing of his throat. Its echo made it sound more powerful than it really was.

"Okay," he began. "Did anyone actually read the assignment?"

What started as a quiet chuckle intensified as students looked around to see if anyone had.

"Well, I guess it would be 'uncool' if you had, so I won't 'call you out' on it."

More laughter.

"Nietzsche can be interpreted in many ways. Obviously, as I discussed last time, the Nazi party interpreted his work in a much different way than we do today. Perspective, of course, has a lot to do with that. Was he way ahead of his time? Some would say that no, in fact, he may have been more comparable to those ancient Greek philosophers we talked about at the beginning of the semester. What was he trying to tell us about the establishment? What was he *really* trying to tell us?"

An arm raised in the back caught his attention.

"Yes?"

"I think he was a really angry guy just trying to make us all feel as bad as he did about how depressing the world is," the male student remarked.

"Depressing, yes, I will agree with that, but why do you think he wrote in the style and tone that he did?"

"He sounds angry," the young man replied. "Like if he lived today, he'd be, like, a shoe-bomber or something."

The room was now filled with laughter as the professor paced behind his podium.

"Well, you know," the professor began while scratching his arm. "Think about the time he lived in. He felt somewhat brought down by the religious establishment. He was fighting to enlighten those that would listen. So perhaps he wrote in such a way that would create some shock value. The anger you interpret may have been an intentional way to get you to read on."

The itch in his arm was intensifying.

"Remember the Communist Manifesto. Remember the way it made you feel when you read it."

Burning.

The same student raised his hand again.

"Yes?"

"It made me feel like I was being brainwashed into starting a riot."

Laughter again.

The professor stopped pacing and gripped the sides of the podium, hoping that if he held on to it tight enough, that he would be able to forget the burning itch that was now crawling up his arm to torture his brain.

"We're all being brainwashed," he growled with obvious discomfort on his face.

Some students shuffled their feet as the room grew silent. The students stared as the professor began to twitch and tap his feet rapidly. He groaned and let his head hang down. He cleared his throat a few times and tried to look up at his class again. The overwhelming itch had taken control.

"Sir?" a student on the first row asked. "Are you all right?"

The student's question seemed to echo through the large room.

"Yes ... just ... give me a moment," he gasped before collapsing into unconsciousness.

Two minutes passed before he came to.

"Where am I?" the Professor asked.

"We called an ambulance for you, sir," a student standing over him replied.

"No!"

The professor jumped to his feet and ran as fast as he could for the door. He avoided the looks on the faces of concerned students and pushed them aside to escape. He had no time to get to his office. He checked his back pocket for his wallet and took a side door to the parking lot.

A flight from Philadelphia to Las Vegas would take just over five hours. He would have to book a room after he got there. And hopefully it would be near the Science Fiction convention that the famous ufologist, Dr. Fitzpatrick, was scheduled to attend.

20

Edward tried not to look obvious while doing it, but he lifted his head from his computer screen every time a person passed by. He wanted to see Mike purposely ignore the open door to his office. He wanted to see what it would be like for Mike to stroll by without jumping through his office on one of his early morning caffeine trips. Edward knew that no one else in the building would pretend to be interested in Mike's stories about all the parties he used to attend before he started working for Corpotex.

"Who designed this spreadsheet?" Edward mumbled before looking up to see Mr. Bennett hovering in front of Anthony's office.

Mr. Bennett poked his head in, turned it from side to side and then backed out. He then turned and started walking into Edward's office. "Hello there, my boy!" he greeted Edward with his good-old-boy flare.

Edward straightened his posture. "Good morning, sir," he replied.

Mr. Bennett chuckled. His shiny brown cowboy boots caught Edward's attention. They were made of some kind of exotic animal.

"Where's your man, Anthony?" Mr. Bennett asked.

"I'm not sure, but I think he stops for coffee on his way up. Is there something you need me to tell him?"

"Oh," Mr. Bennett seemed displaced for a moment. "It's no bother. I guess I can tell you just the same. I'm sending you on a business trip."

Edward's blood coursed through his body slightly faster. "Sir?"

"I need you to go to a conference for me. Kind of like a spy. Some of my biggest competitors have booths set up in Vegas at some software deal. Snoop around and write up some report on your findings. Play like you are interested in investing or somethin' and see if they have some software features that we don't." Mr. Bennett could sense that Edward was worried. "It'll be fun! Las Vegas!"

Edward couldn't think straight. His face flushed. "I don't understand. Why don't you send a guy from the software development team?"

"What?" Mr. Bennett protested. "Are you out of your dang mind? Those boys don't have people skills! Besides, I can't send an expert. I need you to act like you're a guy interested in the stuff. I want them to explain it to you."

"Why don't we set up a booth there also and make some sales?"

Mr. Bennett sighed and looked over Edward's shoulder to watch a flock of birds pass by through the window. "You ask too many questions, son. Your flight leaves tonight. I have a room booked for you and I'll give Anthony all the details you need. You should only be there one night."

"How soon will you be expecting the report?"

"What report?"

"The report on the software convention," Edward reminded him.

"Right. How's Friday sound?" he smiled.

Edward relaxed his jaw but the tension headache had already begun. "It sounds good," he lied.

"Okay then," Mr. Bennett turned to leave Edward to his spreadsheet before stopping suddenly. "Oh, and I need to borrow Anthony while you're gone. Deidra called in sick. Something contagious."

"Okay," he agreed. He stared at Mr. Bennett's back as he walked out the door.

Something didn't feel right. He hadn't seen Mike, Deidra was out sick, and he was being sent out of town. *Las Vegas?* He had to get in touch with Deidra. She knew how these people operated. She could have been a psychopath profiler for some secret government operation because that's how good she was at it, in his eyes.

Edward peeked into the hallway to make sure that Mr. Bennett was heading back down to his office. As soon as he saw him disappear, Edward made a hasty dash toward the elevators. It felt like an escape. Although he didn't think it was good for his mental health to be paranoid, he began rehearsing a cover story in his head. He was just looking for Anthony. That's all. He was going to call Deidra to let her know what was going on and that he was about to freak the hell out.

He could already hear her voice instructing him to calm down. *Can't this elevator go any faster?* She would assure him that he was not being sent there on a hit assignment. *He would have told me, right?* She would jolt him back into reality because for some reason he trusted her. And at the same time, he didn't trust her. *Mr. Bennett wouldn't pick me. Franklin's practically my long lost dad.*

Edward's fast-paced walk through the parking garage became a sprint until he made it to his car. He clumsily dropped the keys, picked them up, dropped them again, pressed the wrong button, set the alarm off, then got inside and took a moment to catch his breath. He had to call her.

"Hello?" she answered hesitantly.

"Hey! What are you doing? What happened to 'see you on Monday'?" he mimicked.

"I'm sick. Sorry," she said without even trying to fake the illness she didn't have.

"They're sending me out of town!" he panicked into the phone.

First she was silent. Then she gasped. "Where are you calling me from!"

"Inside my car."

"There's a pharmacy by my apartment. Do you remember how to get here?" A fake cough then came through.

"Yes, sort of," he answered. "It's not like I drive by there all the time ... stalking you or anything." He swallowed uncomfortably.

"I have to get some medicine for this. I don't feel good at all. It would be nice if you could come over here and get some flu symptom stuff for me. I can meet you at the gate first to tell you what kind to get," she explained carefully.

Edward couldn't tell if she was being serious or covering something up but he went along with it anyway.

"See you soon," she said and ended the call.

"But I ..." Edward pressed his back hard into the car seat and grimaced. He scrolled through his contacts list as fast as he could and called Anthony.

"Hello, sir," Anthony said.

"Anthony!" Edward rejoiced. "Where are you?"

"I'm in my office arranging your flight itinerary."

"When do I leave?"

"Tonight at 7:30."

Edward cringed. "Okay, look, I need to get some things together before tonight. This is kind of short notice for me and ..."

"No problem, sir. Take the rest of the day to get things in order. I will have everything ready when you get to the airport. I will meet you at the check-in desk."

"Okay."

"I will see you around 6:30, Mr. Bloodgood."

21

Edward pulled up to the front of Deidra's apartment complex. The landscaping was perfect. It was meant to present itself as a visual feast for refined eyes. More than plants alone situated into a symmetrical design, it was a presentation meant to aesthetically please while at the same time make you want to pay too much for rent.

Deidra's car pulled up and stopped just inside the gate. She practically pushed through the gate as it opened at a crawl. She pulled up alongside him and waved for him to get inside her car. He pulled his car closer to the curb so it would be out of the way, and got inside hers.

She wore designer sweats. He knew this only because he had recently learned to see clothing differently than before. Being around her did that to him. She did not appear to be ill in any way. Her makeup was perfect and her hair was as silky and as perfectly set as usual.

"What's going on?" he asked. "Are you really sick?"

"Maybe. And I don't trust your car."

She drove them to the parking lot of the pharmacy, turned off the car, and looked him over. "Take off your jacket."

Edward grinned. "It's about time you asked me to do that."

"I'm not joking. Take off the jacket."

Edward complied and after several spastic motions, was able to remove it and hand it to Deidra. She patted it and inspected its pockets meticulously. Her fingers slid and pressed against every fiber. She felt the lining and crumpled sections of it in her hands.

"I'm not going to make you take your pants off, but I want you to get out and feel inside your pockets, then pat yourself down," she commanded.

Edward's eyelids began to flutter as he rolled his eyes back into his head. He stepped out of the car with exaggerated sarcasm in his limbs.

"Can you please take this seriously?" she scolded. "And try to look natural."

He twisted his lips and did exactly as she had instructed. Deidra watched, eyes wide. When she was satisfied, she waved him back inside.

"People probably think I was making out with myself," he added. "Thanks."

"Give me your cell phone," she said. She held her palm out to him.

Edward handed it over. She opened her car window and set it on top of the roof of the car, rolled the window back up, and smiled.

"Okay," she was ready to get down to business. "I think they're sending you out of town to make sure you have no connection or contact with Mike."

"It's as simple as that?" Edward wasn't buying it at all.

"Yes." she said with caution. "But just to make sure, I called in sick to follow him."

Edward closed his eyes and pressed his temples with his fingers. "This is just ... I can't understand this crap." He inhaled through his nostrils hoping that more oxygen to the brain might help.

"I've been thinking about it and I can't let it go. Besides, wouldn't you feel better if I could prove to you that it's not your job?"

"But I thought we already did that! You said it couldn't be me!" he exploded.

"What's going on with you and Franklin?" she asked harshly. "Ever since you've been around he's become distant. I know it has something to do with you so spill it!"

Edward was too embarrassed to explain it to her. How could he admit to her that Franklin supported him and his mother his entire life. He didn't know anything about her childhood. Why should he embarrass himself? No matter how hard he tried to figure her out, she had no past. He felt close to her at times, but only because she was his guide. She was his window into the disgusting, disappointing, horrible truths he never would have known. "He dated my mom in high school." Edward lowered his head. "He paid my way through college. Don't worry, he's not my dad. Thank God."

"What?"

"Yeah. I was really poor growing up, but I guess Franklin felt sorry for us so we became one of his charities," Edward spoke with a bite.

Deidra turned to him and placed a hand on his knee. "It's all right. I'm sorry I asked like that, but it does explain something." She was gentle.

"What?"

"I think Franklin is taking extra care to keep you out of this. He wants you far away. Just go along with it. Congratulations. You're being protected."

Edward laughed. "How refreshing."

"Can you go inside now and buy some cold medicine? Don't forget your phone up there," she pointed. "And some gummy bears!"

He knew the routine. He was going to do what she said no matter how pointless it was to him. As much as he joked about her overly cautious personality, in his mind, she was still more experienced than he was. He wasn't going to try and prevent her from following Mike. It was her firm contention that a world-changing atrocity was in progress with Mike as the gunman. Deidra had found her moral calling and something was feeding her desire to learn more about it.

22

The only way Edward could think to get himself through the non-stop flight to Vegas was to start drinking as soon as the plane took off. The child sitting in front of him kept turning around, peeking through the cracks of the seats. After two bourbon and cokes, Edward flipped him the bird.

"Mommy! That man showed me the bad finger!" the kid wailed.

Edward stretched in his seat, amused with himself. Las Vegas wouldn't be so bad. If the trip really was another pointless assignment thrown his way to keep him busy, why not enjoy it? At that moment, not unlike many others, Edward was wishing that Deidra was his assistant. Her first order of business would be to accompany him to Vegas. The second order would be to smack the kid sitting in front of them.

After a couple of hours of building castles out of clear plastic cups, his plane landed in the hot desert of Nevada. He was met near baggage claim by a driver that discreetly walked up to him and asked if he could carry his luggage to the car. Edward was pleasantly surprised, and glad that he had invested in a new set of luggage.

The hotel was over-the-top in elegance and equally in glamour. Edward checked in at the desk and asked about the software convention. He was provided with brochures and a door key. The conference was already in progress. He had his things taken to his room, quickly washed his face, and headed back down towards the event.

The conference was as boring as he expected. But, Edward was onto them. He could see that the nerd world conspiracy was in full effect. They had created programs and upgrades to programs in an attempt to gain control of the business world. These nerds had apparently told the salespeople working the booths to answer 'yes' to every question asked by anyone even remotely interested in their products. Of course the software was full-proof, would increase productivity, was bug-free, and would only be understood after reading the 500 page user's manual.

More nerds would then have to be hired in nerd-teams to set up training classes for the multitudes of employees that would be using the software to perform their essential job duties. As soon as every single employee understood the detailed functions of the software product, an upgrade would be available that the business would not be able to live without, thus requiring more teams of nerds to be paid for re-training. Edward guessed that the nerds would one day rise and trigger some dormant line of code hidden inside millions of companies computers' and set forth the end of times.

Where's that lady with the tray of bourbon?

He could feel the energy vibrations of technology trying to gain control of his brain. Then a vibration started from within his jacket. "Hello?" he answered his cell phone.

"Where are you?" Deidra asked.

"I'm in Vegas, baby! Woo hoo!" he yelled into the phone. The murmurs of salespeople and buyers were drowning out his voice.

"Are you checked in and stuff?"

"Yes. I'm almost on my sixth drink," he boasted. "How's being sick going?"

"Fine. Hey, listen. There's a weird convention going on in the hotel next to yours. Did you see the sign for it outside?"

"No," Edward didn't care. She probably wanted a souvenir. "I'm trying to find that lady with the tray ..."

"Eddie. Focus. I need you to tell me the name of the convention next to your hotel."

"What the fuck? What am I to you?" Edward complained as he set his empty glass down and walked toward the lobby of his hotel. "Some kind of sign-reading directory guy? You think I came all the way to Vegas to read things? Hell no! I came here to gamble and drink and look at girls and ..."

Edward was standing just outside the casino. He pushed through the large glass doors and looked around at the massive hotels surrounding him. "What hotel convention?" He stopped and looked to his right. He could see Deidra waving her arms at him under a banner that read 'Welcome to The 10th Annual Science Fiction Convention'.

"You're stupid," she informed him with a laugh before disconnecting the call.

Edward rushed over to greet her. She smiled happily as he approached in an awkward swaying motion, his arms folded. "What are you doing here?" he scolded in a sing-song voice that made Deidra cringe.

"Wow. You need some coffee, drunk-ass." She made a quick assessment of him and then looked at her watch. "Let's get to your room."

She tugged him by the arm and led them up to his room. There was a skull on her shirt and the word 'Danzig' written across her chest. He was happy to see her in a rock t-shirt and some jeans instead of her usual business attire. Edward stopped along the way only to pull his card key from his pocket and then once more to gawk at a slot machine that flashed in an array of colors advertising its high payout. Deidra had to shove him into the elevator to separate him from the poetic chaos that was the typical Las Vegas hotel casino.

"It's like a grown-up theme park. With alcohol and hookers," Edward panted as Deidra pulled him through the door and into his room.

"Have you actually seen any hookers since you've been here?" she teased.

"No." He pouted.

"Eddie, you really need to sober up. You've only been here for how long?" She reminded him. "An hour? How did you get messed up so fast?" She pulled the curtains closed.

"I started on the plane." He flopped onto the bed. "Why are you here?"

"Well, this is the thing about you being drunk that sucks. I really need you to be sober so I can explain that to you."

Edward burst into laughter and spit on himself in the process. "Oh my God! I can't believe I have to shop for software in the morning! That's going to be hilarious! You wanna go with?"

"Edward," she began.

"Or do you just wanna hang out in here and look at my hot body?" He laughed harder than before. "Come on, Deidra. I won't charge you."

She looked at him like he was too pathetic to slap. "Jesus, you are really stupid when you are wasted."

She turned toward the coffee maker sitting in the corner and began to brew an entire pot. Edward watched as she moved about the room in a blur. She was pacing frantically, stopping occasionally to look up to the ceiling. The blurs she kept making started to make him nauseous. Edward realized just how intoxicated he was. Then it suddenly hit him. She would not have come to Vegas without a reason. "What's going on?" he asked, feeling himself sobering rapidly.

Deidra looked at him and worry rushed over her face. "He's here. I followed Mike and he's here," she said with haunting emphasis on the word 'here'.

"What? But I'm not involved! Why is the job here?" Edward was filled with the urge to run, but knew he couldn't. The overwhelming fear of death numbed him. Whomever was about to die, he didn't want to see it, be near it, be in the same town with it, or hear about it in any way. He had convinced himself on the plane that Franklin was his mystical guardian—the protector of Edward. He couldn't face death, or Mike.

"I don't know anymore, Eddie," she admitted. "I thought I had it figured out, at least part of it, but I don't."

"Are they trying to implicate me?" he panicked. "You know … same place, same time type of thing? Why would they do that to me?"

"Exactly," she agreed. "I don't think they would …"

Deidra froze.

"What?" He jumped at the sight of her face. She was like a statue. Her face went pale instantly. She pointed a shaky finger to an area behind him on the bed. "What is that?"

He turned as fast as he could and saw it. A small suitcase sat on top of a pillow on the bed, unlocked and waiting for its contents to be discovered. Edward immediately scooted off the bed and stood next to her while also trying to get away from the suitcase.

"Open it," she dared him.

"No way."

"You're supposed to. Mr. Bennett had this room booked for you in advance. This was left for you," she explained. "They probably know I'm here, too." She bent down to open her handbag and grabbed a sweater. She pulled it on as fast as she could and looked out the large window.

Edward, sure that it would be the end of his plans for drinking and gambling all night, approached the suitcase and lifted its lid with one finger. It popped open with a bounce to reveal a gun and an envelope. "Shit."

Deidra lost her footing and caught herself on the edge of the bed. "It's you? I don't get it … open the envelope!"

Edward moved the gun aside with his elbow and peeled the flap of the envelope open. It was the same style of envelope he had seen at the race. He knew it would be different from any envelope he would ever open.

His eyes skimmed its paper contents and he pursed his lips together. "Well," he prepared her. "They want me to kill someone. There's only a room number and then some disgusting instructions for what to do with ... the body."

"Who do they want you to kill?"

"It doesn't say. It just says to kill the person in the room with one bullet, or I'll be killed."

Deidra placed her hands to her temples. "This is unreal!" She massaged the side of her head. "Do you want me to do it for you?" she asked as if she was offering to wash his car.

"No! I mean, yes, but no. Won't they kill me if you do it?"

"They have to know I am here. I'm probably a better shot than you anyway," she began to present her case for taking over the assignment while walking up to him with a finger on her lip. "I know you're new to this stuff and I'm sure Mike is just some kind of a backup that was sent to make sure the job was done correctly. We all work for the same man, technically. It's no big deal. I'll do it for you if you want me to."

She leaned in close to his ear and whispered, "They're listening." She then continued to speak normally. "So I guess they know about us then."

Edward knew where she was leading him and played along. "I guess so."

"We should just play it cool for now." She scanned the perimeter of the room, sure that if the assignment was important enough, they would have bugged the room.

Edward stared at the paper in his hand. "I have to get this done in less than an hour. By 9:45."

"Let's get some food and then come back and get ready ..."

Edward's mind was racing. "We have ... I have less than an hour to prepare myself mentally to kill a person!"

"Edward! I'm hungry! Let's eat and then come back," she fixed her eyes into a wild fury and yanked on his sleeve desperately.

Edward understood. "Eat fast."

They grabbed two cups of coffee and a couple of doughnuts at a café set up in the lobby before settling down in front of two slot machines in the hotel's casino. They placed their coffees next to the machines and ate as Deidra continuously placed twenties into the colorful slots in front of them. Edward's body was alive with nervous electricity. He fidgeted and tapped his feet on the carpet. The spinning shapes Deidra kept staring at made him feel dizzy. That night would be the last he would spend as an innocent bystander.

"Maybe Mike's a decoy," she suggested without looking away from her game. "I didn't want to talk about it in the room. The Mike part of this really confuses me."

"And you were so sure that they wouldn't try to get me to do it."

"You need to eat that doughnut faster. It will help sober you up."

"Trust me, I'm sober."

"When you told me about your connection to Franklin, I started thinking that you might be the one, but ..."

"What about protecting me? What happened to that theory?"

"I was wrong, okay? Get over it! Grow the fuck up and face the job you have been given." She was angry at him for being so afraid. "I'm not wrong very often."

"Great," Edward sighed. He put a twenty in and won forty dollars in return. The sound of sirens went off and lights flashed.

"I was wrong once before," she began. "It was in Del Rio, Texas. Have you ever been there?"

"I just won forty bucks."

"It's on the border. It looks like a regular small town but it's not. It has secrets. Never forget that. Never."

"Shouldn't we go?"

"Yeah. Let's collect your money and go."

$$\approx \sim \delta$$

"What about the job? Should I just do it?" he asked as they neared the elevator.

"Tell me what the instructions said specifically."

Edward recoiled at the thought of it. The paper inside the brown envelope was a nightmare inducing list of things he had nothing to compare to. He was expected to carry out these instructions or his own life was at stake. It didn't feel any better to him that Deidra, playing the twisted detective, wanted to get involved more than she already was. Instead of catching the next flight out of Vegas to distance herself from it all, she had appointed herself as his partner.

"They said that at 9:45 I'm supposed to enter the room using the card key inside the briefcase and shoot someone inside one time in the head. Then, I'm supposed to," Edward closed his eyes, "cut off the right arm."

"Wow."

"Not 'wow.' Gross," he corrected.

"Can I go?" she pleaded.

"This isn't a field trip, Deidra. It's a crime."

"Yeah, but I want to help!"

He looked at his watch in haste. "Look, you know these kinds of things better than I do. If you can handle seeing this stuff ..."

"Of course I can handle it! They know I'm helping you. They have to know. If they didn't want me here, my plane would have gone down or someone would have poisoned this doughnut," she argued with a half-eaten doughnut in hand.

Edward shook his head, truly afraid for her sanity. "You have a very strange outlook on things."

"My dad was in the intelligence business," she explained. "Everyone is out to get you, they are always watching, and nothing is a coincidence."

23

Once back in the room, Edward compared the time on his watch to the time on the digital clock on the nightstand. They both read 9:35.

Deidra watched in silence as Edward grabbed the gun from the suitcase and placed it inside his coat pocket. He folded the brown envelope into the size of an index card. He stood for a moment, closing his eyes and collecting his thoughts and placed the envelope into his pants pocket. She loved watching a prep. It was an emotional rush that she could not explain to anyone. One just had to go through it themselves to know. The experience of it was like a drug to her and to live it from the outside, when it wasn't her own prep, was surreal.

Edward headed for the door.

Deidra, as if invisible, moved behind him as he made his way back to the elevator they had just come from. Inside, she stood away from him, hoping that some personal space might help to keep him focused on the task at hand. This definitely wasn't the time for second guessing.

The elevator moved and his eyes blurred as he stared at the illuminated circular button he had selected. The rectangular box they were standing in was taking them to the ninth floor. The effects of alcohol were long gone and the sting of reality had taken over. He was once the boy who watched his mother as she primped and preened herself before work. He idolized her and had no idea that most ten-year-old boys didn't know the difference between the various types of mascaras. He had no clue that boys weren't supposed to know what concealer was and what it was used to conceal. All he understood at the time was that she seemed to be hiding herself under layers of liquid foundation, powder, and shimmery toppings, but he could not figure out why.

The elevator stopped at the sound of a ding. The doors opened and Edward stepped out, head hanging down, and with Deidra following close behind.

When he reached the midway point of the long carpeted hallway, he glanced at one of the room number plaques as he passed it. Realizing that he was close to his destination, Edward slowed his pace. Deidra nearly ran into him, but caught herself and scanned the hallway for activity. She was looking for witnesses.

It was 9:41.

"What time is it?" she whispered over his shoulder.

"We have time. It's two doors from here."

His calm demeanor was nerve-racking to her. It wasn't his usual freak out mode. Or his prissy sissy mode that she was used to. "Good idea. We should stay back until it's time. Maybe we should wait down by the elevator ..."

"No."

"Eddie, are you all right?"

The elevator door opened and an elderly couple appeared. The man did his best to push his walker out through the large metal doors without making a commotion, but the sides of it clanged against them. The green-colored tennis balls that were attached to the walker's front metal legs were distracting. The man's wife moved around him and into the hallway's entrance, placing herself in a position to help guide him and the walker out with care. He refused her help, waving her away. "Get your hands off," the man warned her. Their bickering voices carried toward Edward and Deidra.

"How are you supposed to get in?" Deidra asked.

He pulled the folded envelope from his pants pocket. He unfolded and opened it carefully to reveal the card key inside.

He held the card firmly with one hand while placing his other hand on the side of his jacket. He slid his hand down and felt the handle of the gun.

"What were you going to do? Wait until the last minute to get that thing out?" she looked at the couple as they made virtually no progress to their room. "What is taking them so long?"

Edward's watch read 9:42.

"Give me the key," she demanded quickly. "I'll open the door when you say, then we'll run in."

"I'm going to shoot those old people if they don't get inside their room in two minutes." His eyes were glassy and his brain worked to ease the tension collecting around his temples.

"Give me the key!"

"No."

"Why not?"

"Shut up! Just follow me in and stay quiet! My God, you're having a good time, aren't you? This is really exciting to you, isn't it? I don't want to do this, but it's my job so let me fucking do it!" he hissed. He felt an insanity swimming inside him.

Deidra took a step backwards and then turned to look at the white-haired couple. They had stopped to look for their card key. The woman was arguing with the man about whether or not they were on the wrong floor. She knew Edward was doing his best to remain in control. She would endure his machismo tantrum until the whole thing was over. Then she would let him have it.

"Eddie, I think those old people aren't going anywhere so we're just going to have to try and look natural and go in."

Edward smirked in her direction and then checked his watch. 9:43. "Look natural. That's a good one."

The old man handed his wife the wallet from his back pocket and challenged her to look through it for the elusive key before scooting his walker down the hallway and closer to where Edward and Deidra were standing. When the old woman found the key she scurried to catch up to her grumpy partner. She mumbled curses at his back.

Deidra placed a hand on Edward's shoulder and pulled him back slightly. "Their room is right behind us."

Edward turned to see the old man set his walker down right in front of the room they were standing across from. The old man then turned and looked at them.

"You two married?" the man asked.

"Uh ... no," Deidra replied.

"Good for you," the man praised. "If I wasn't stuck with this witch, I would be much happier. And she used to be good-looking, too!"

Edward nodded his head quickly in absent agreement and turned back to face the door he and Deidra were hovering in front of. *Get inside your room already you old waste of...*

"You be sure to treat him right," the old man advised Deidra.

"Oh, leave them alone," his wife demanded. "They don't want your advice."

"I'm just trying to save the poor man from a life of hell."

"Young people don't want your help, Floyd. They want to have fun with people their own age. They want to go dancing and ..." the woman turned to them with an inquisitive look on her face. "How you young people do all that breakdancing without hurting yourselves, I will never know."

Deidra clutched Edward's arm and buried her face into the back part of his shoulder to muffle her snickering. Edward wasn't amused. He broke from Deidra's grip and turned to stand close to the elderly couple. "Do you need help getting into your room?" he asked impatiently. "Is this your room? 954?"

"Yes it is. We can get in just fine, thank you," the woman said before finally figuring out how to get her card key to open their door.

They disappeared inside room 954, still bickering on the way in.

Edward then slid the card key he held between the slots anchored to the door, and entered. A man sitting on the edge of a king sized bed watched in horror as a gun was aimed at his face by a man he had never seen before. Deidra entered the room just behind Edward and immediately stepped into the bathroom and closed the door. She wanted to do whatever she could to stay out of Edward's way.

The man sitting at the end of the bed raised both arms into the air and looked at Edward in fear. Edward could tell that the man wanted to speak. He sat quietly waiting for the man with the gun to tell him what he wanted. The man wore his hair in a ponytail behind his back. Thin, round-framed glasses accented his face and a short neatly kept goatee finished off his post-hippy style. He was going to try to reason with the gun-wielding man. It was his deep belief that everyone had a conscience.

"Please," the man started. "You don't know what's happening here. Don't hurt me."

Edward couldn't listen. He couldn't look at the man as a person. He had to black out the human element and convince himself that this was nothing more than a job. It had to be done. "Don't talk."

"Please," the man fell from the bed and then onto his knees on the floor below. The science fiction themed shirt he wore was of a movie Edward didn't recognize. "I know that whoever hired you to do this did not tell you the truth. If you kill me … you could be endangering the lives of millions! Billions! The fate of the world depends on …"

"I said don't talk!" The gun shook in Edward's grasp. *Maybe the guy is a monster. Don't listen to him.*

"If you let me go, I can contact people who can pay you more."

The man's voice was interrupted by the sound of a click and the swift motion of the room's door being forced open from the outside. Edward swung around, his weapon now aimed at their new guest as he entered. It was Mike. The only thing more distracting than the brightly-colored Hawaiian shirt Mike was wearing was the gun in his hand, pointed at Edward.

The two of them stood facing one another at gunpoint. The man on his knees behind Edward didn't know if he should prepare himself for death or if the second man wearing the horrible shirt was his savior.

"What's up?" Mike asked Edward, breaking the eerie silence.

"I have no idea," he replied in frustration. Edward couldn't understand it. Had the two of them both been sent to kill this man?

Mike cocked his head to one side and smiled. He looked around the room, caught the eye of the man at the foot of the bed, and then focused his attention back onto his ex-roommate. "You haven't figured it out yet?"

"Figured out what?"

"I'm sorry I had to kick you out of the apartment, Eddie. But it's all a part of the game," Mike said while taking a moment to glance at his wrist watch. "Well, are you going to kill that guy or what?"

"Why are you here, Mike?" Edward had a bad feeling about the scenario. Two guns in the same room during a hit didn't seem to add up nicely.

"To kill *you*."

It made sense. Although he was a bit shaken by the idea of being shot, it seemed only logical that he, too, would be targeted for murder at some point. Like Mike said, it was a game. They were playing with death. To Edward, it was comparable to losing his virginity. Once he finally got laid, he hoped sex would become a regular thing in his life and thought about it more than he had as a virgin. The only difference was that the element of murder reversed things a bit. He knew that once he murdered someone for these people, they would probably ask him to do it again. And so unlike sex, he wanted to get the job done and never think about. He hadn't expected Mike to interrupt him like this. It threw a kink in things.

"Why am I supposed to die? I don't even see how that fits into any of this?" he asked calmly, not believing that Mike could kill him so easily and also remembering that Deidra was hiding nearby.

"I'm just doing my job." Mike's expression was cold.

"Are you killing me to save this guy?" Edward wondered, sure that Deidra was listening carefully.

The guy at the foot of the bed smiled, looking toward the heavens.

"No," Mike answered.

The man on his knees frowned.

"So, I kill him and then you kill me? Why?" Edward asked.

"Look," Mike reset his footing to get comfortable for a moment while explaining. "I don't give a fuck about the order of things. I can kill you first if that's how you want it."

"What the hell is this about? Who's the bad guy then? Me, you, or him?"

"I don't have time to talk all night, Eddie. Just shoot the guy and …"

"Please!" the man on the floor interrupted with a screeching whine. "Let me tell you what's going on. This is a big mistake. The fate of the planet …"

"Shut up!" Mike turned his aim away from Edward's chest and shot the man behind him in the forehead. The man slumped forward, his lifeless body making a thud on the hotel floor. Blood oozed around his face, the dark puddle spilling and reaching out in the direction of Edward's shoes.

Edward stepped forward instinctively as the wave of blood crept closer to his heals. He looked up at Mike just in time to see Deidra closing in behind him with a hair dryer raised above her head. Mike toppled to the ground as the hair dryer slammed against the top of his skull. Mike rolled quickly onto his back, attempting to point his gun at the unseen attacker but it was kicked out of his hand by Deidra's shoe. She dove to the right and over Mike onto the bed behind Edward. Mike's hand grabbed her ankle and Edward swung around, taking care not to look at the blood soaking on the floor. He grabbed Mike's gun and then stood erect, pointing both guns at him. "Let go of her!"

Reluctantly, Mike released his grip on Deidra. After she corrected her balance, Edward handed her Mike's weapon. She stood over Mike and aimed the gun at his face.

"Who do you work for?" she asked.

"Fuck you, whore."

"I'm going to kill you, Mike. You might as well tell me who it is before I do." She positioned the gun closer to his face with a steady two-handed grip.

Mike stayed silent.

"Close your eyes, Eddie," she cautioned him before waiting only a moment to pull the trigger.

Edward watched as she searched Mike's clothing. She sat still for a moment and then looked back at the other man face down on the floor. There just wasn't enough time to prepare him to finish this job. It had been one horrific thing after the next with no commercial breaks in between like he was used to.

"He was a company man. I know it," she muttered.

"Just so you know ... I didn't close my eyes."

"You lived with this guy. You had no idea he was CIA?"

Edward could swear that he smelled blood. *Can you actually smell blood?* The room surrounded him in death. He had to shake himself from the nightmare before it overwhelmed him.

"Isn't it funny how you still haven't killed anyone? It's like a bad joke or something." Deidra stood and then breathed deeply. "What's next? The arm thing?"

"Yeah." *The arm thing.*

He turned to see her holding something that looked like rolled up fabric. "What is that?"

"I found it on Mike. It's a bunch of surgical tools." She stared at him expectantly. "Do what you have to do because we can't hang around here long. You know? They call it 'shots fired' on 911 calls."

He had to think for a moment before remembering what to do exactly. He went out of his way to avoid looking at Mike's face or the gaping hole in his head, but also had to get over his body to get to the bathroom. Once there, he knelt down in front of the sink and opened the cabinet doors underneath. He tilted his head to look inside and found what he was looking for scrunched up and duct-taped to the side wall. It was a duffle bag wrapped around a piece of silver wire.

Edward rose to his feet with a groan. He could hear Deidra moving something around next to the bed. He stepped out of the bathroom in a trance-like state, preparing himself for the next step.

Deidra stood over the body of the man Mike shot for them. She had repositioned the body so that it was facing upward. It was now sprawled out and unnaturally contorted.

"I thought it would be easier to cut that way," she said.

"Right," he agreed with disappointment.

Edward maneuvered himself around Mike's body and stood over what was now his unfinished assignment. He tossed the crumpled plastic duffel bag onto the bed and then studied the wire in his hands. He had seen it in a few movies he now wished he hadn't watched. He knew exactly how to hook the ends of the wire to the handles provided. He could see the sawing motion it would make against the arm in his mind.

"Wow. That's what they gave you to do it with?" She couldn't control her excitement. "Gigli wire?"

"Yeah, but I don't think I can do it. I'm trying to psych myself up. I've seen it in movies, but they don't ever really show that part of it. It's always implied. And then you can't believe that someone would actually do that to another person. I mean except for a doctor, I guess, but they are used to it."

"Uh, Eddie? Aren't we in a hurry?"

"Okay." He held the handles firmly and knelt down to one knee. He was careful not to look into the contorted face of the man he was about to amputate. His breathing became steady and in the silence of the room he could hear the buzz of electricity vibrating within the walls.

Edward held his outstretched arms above the man's right arm and pulled the saw wire tight and ready, but the tightness in his chest and throat prevented him from moving in to begin. He wondered if he should pull up his sleeves first. Then he wondered if he should check the man's pulse before starting. Just in case.

She eyed him with impatience and wondered why Edward had been chosen to carry out this gruesome task. He didn't have the savage thirst for blood, or any of other things that would be required to carry this type of thing out.

"I'll do it," she offered with a gentle voice.

He felt ashamed and relieved at the same time.

"Just get the bag ready and some towels to wrap it in." She smiled a faint smile that warmed him. "And you can stay in the bathroom if you want to until I'm finished."

24

She stood before him in the bathroom doorway, clutching the handles of the bag. "I had to wrap it in the towels and then used a plastic bag to seal it."

Edward felt dizzy. She had removed the arm so fast that guilt had not had its chance yet to take a hold of him. Just nausea.

"Come on. We have to get it out of here. Get off the floor," she urged.

As he rose, he could see her swinging the bag toward him.

"I'm going to go ahead downstairs and I'll meet up with you when you get to the lobby," she explained as she handed him the bag. "Here."

He grabbed the bag from her and was immediately surprised with how light its contents felt. Before Edward could say anything to her, Deidra was out of the room and heading for the casino area.

It would be tricky, but he had to figure out a way to get down the hall and into the elevator discreetly. Surely nobody would know that he was carrying a severed arm, but he wasn't very good at playing things off. He didn't have a poker face.

The next part of his instructions said to get a taxi and take it to the address written on the piece of paper inside the envelope. All he had to do was open the door and force himself into the long hallway. He took a moment to rub the bottoms of his shoes against the carpet before exiting the room. *I know what will happen. The maid will scream when she opens the door.*

The trek toward the elevator would have been more peaceful if he could have controlled his pounding heart and heavy breaths. His body mechanics were in a state of total disarray. Beads of sweat started to run down his face. He quickened his pace, made it through the elevator doors, and pressed the button for the lobby. He leaned back against the mirrored wall, holding the duffle bag away from his side. He imagined what a real murderer would do in his situation and then carefully allowed the bag to hang loosely next to his leg.

As the doors opened and he was released into the wild lights and sounds of the hotel casino, he set course for the street outside. He spotted Deidra hanging up on a phone call at the check-in desk. She hurried toward him.

"I know a place we can go," she said casually while working to pace herself alongside his brisk speed. She placed a hand on his arm, suggesting that he slow down. He carried the bag level and didn't allow for it to sway naturally the way she thought it should.

"I have a place to go. It's in the instructions."

"That's what I need to talk to you about," she said as she stepped ahead of him to hold open the glass door at the entrance. They walked out into the night and Edward looked up to see the sky decorated with street lights and the glow that came from every building surrounding them. She clutched his arm just above the elbow and smiled. "Look at me."

"What?"

"We have to take a taxi to this place outside of Vegas ..."

"I have to take a taxi to the address in my pocket or someone's going to fucking kill me!" His voice was cold.

Deidra let go of him and jumped in front of his face. She stood up on her toes trying to be at eye level with him. She needed him to listen to her and knew that it was going to be a difficult task. He feared for his life. It was exactly how those in charge had planned it. "There's something inside that arm."

Edward frowned. "What?" he asked sarcastically.

She moved in closer, placing her arm around his neck. Making sure that to anyone watching, they were a couple deeply in love. "I felt something inside the arm. There's a bump on the skin. Something had been ... implanted there. There's a tiny scar, too."

He listened, unaffected by her secret agent tactics. He was too preoccupied with following instructions and staying alive. "What are you saying?"

"I'm saying that we have an obligation to society to try and find out what's going on here. We should get into the taxi and go to the place I want to go to instead of the place you want to go to." Her fake smile and kicked up heal were now complimentary to a flirtatious type of voice that irritated him beyond belief. He doubted seriously that every move they made was under surveillance. The surveillance she imagined was probably nothing more than one or two guys situated back in the lobby riding the clock with a few drinks in hand. But Deidra was pretty sure that the men on the roof of the hotel across the street would disagree, along with the few hotel guests stumbling around near them pretending to be inebriated. The doorman had his eye on them as well.

"I'm going to do what the paper says."

She leaned in even closer, pressing her body against his chest. "There's something inside the arm. Don't let them have it." She pressed harder, moving her hand down his hip and onto his inner thigh.

"What are we going to do with it?" he managed to whisper into a yell while fighting the sensations of arousal shooting through him.

She breathed heavy into his ear, "We'll open it up and see what's inside."

"Then what?" he asked, swallowing back his quickened breaths. Her hand was moving in closer to him and her breath was hot in his ear.

"We'll figure that part out when it's time."

His frustration was over-boiling. "I don't care what it is! Just get off of me. This is stupid!"

She backed away and looked into his eyes. He could see the desperation in them. She was doing everything in her power to restrain herself. She wanted to snatch the bag from his hand and run. The severed arm was her key into another world. It held answers to questions Edward would never ask of life. But they were the answers to questions she had committed her life to finding answers to.

"Okay." She looked behind her and waived for a taxi. "I'm going."

"Where?"

"Somewhere without you."

It wasn't like him to break from the mold. The world presented itself to him and he accepted it. There was no questioning it or any sort of conspiracy-fueled speculation necessary. It was what it was and he had always been comfortable with that.

There was no denying that recent weeks had changed him. Emotions that had never surfaced before ran wild within him, exposing who he was to everyone around him. When he was in the company of these criminals, he was different than he used to be. And when he was in *her* company things turned chaotic.

She stood a few yards from him, glancing back in disapproval. He knew that to her he was nothing but a conformist. The system had a hold of him. He was their tool. What could be so special about that arm? She could have imagined the object she felt. And if there was something implanted inside of it, it wasn't his business to know about it anyway.

He looked down at the black duffle bag and then back at Deidra. A taxi pulled up to the curb before him and waited for some acknowledgement from Edward.

"Come on." She waived to him to join her at her taxi.

He rushed over excitedly, but also scared for their lives. He stepped inside the cab. "This is crazy."

He knew at that moment that he was finished. There couldn't possibly be a way to run from the all-knowing. If these people were as corrupt and as powerful as Deidra made them out to be, his number was certainly up. And so was hers.

"Can you take us to McCarran?" she asked. "Quickly?"

"Sure can," the driver replied as he started the meter.

Edward placed the duffle bag on the floor next to his feet and leaned in close to her ear. "What if it's just a tracking device?"

"It's not," she answered him back. She was confident that she was on to something extraordinary. They were risking their lives to find out either way.

"What's at McCarran?" he wondered.

"Airplanes."

❧

Their taxi dropped them off at the airport entrance and Deidra pulled Edward through the crowds of people standing outside. "Someone's going to meet us here."

"Who?"

"A man."

"Okay."

She led them to the side of the building away from the hectic bustle at the main entrance. She searched the area for the man. From where they stood, he could see twinkling lights on the mountains behind the airport.

"Who is this man?"

"He's going to take us to Pahrump."

"What's that?"

She twisted her lip and glared at him. "It's a town. I chose the airport as a distraction. It might throw off anyone that is following us."

"Where is Pahrump?"

"About an hour from here."

"What are we going to do there?" He felt panic coming on.

"We're going to look at the arm."

He could feel the knot in his throat coming back. "How?"

"We're going to open it with Mike's surgical tools."

It was what he had expected. Only she could be so nonchalant about digging through a dead guy's arm that she herself had removed with a piece of mobster-movie wire. "Do you know people there?"

"In Pahrump? No, but my father does. I called him in the lobby."

"Yeah, I saw you on the phone."

"I told him that I was in some trouble with a friend and that it was something big. I asked him if he knew anyone in Las Vegas and he said he didn't trust anyone in Vegas. He told me to go to the airport and wait for a man to take us to Pahrump to meet a Native American man named Sam."

"Sam?" he asked. The name sounded too plain. It just wasn't what he would have envisioned for the first time he got to meet a person with such an interesting heritage.

"His real name has something to do with the moon but my father said to call him 'Sam.'" She explained further.

"Well, all right then. This all sounds great."

A black car pulled up alongside them and a short man stepped out onto the street and looked over the top of his vehicle at them. The car was still running. "You going to Pahrump?"

"Yes," Deidra exclaimed as she grabbed Edward's arm and forced them through the back door of the car.

Edward felt something wet against his leg as he sat. He looked down at his pant leg and then immediately at the bag he had just set at his feet and shivered. "I think we've got a leak," he groaned. "I'm going to throw up."

"Here." She leaned over and moved the bag to her feet. "You'll be fine. It's just a little spot," she said, referring to the blood on his thigh.

Her voice soothed him. "You're like the school nurse. Maybe you can breathe in my ear again for a while?"

She laughed and the car pulled away from the airport. They took Highway 160 west along a route that led through the Blue Diamond area. Edward wouldn't have noticed the scenery during the drive because he was too busy wondering what would happen to him now that he had abandoned the instructions for the job. The night was calm and the cactus along the road mocked him. Many of them looked like they were flipping him off, their bodies taking on the shape of middle fingers on large hands. He wondered if they would throw his body out among them later.

"Thank you," she said so that he would turn to look at her.

"For what?"

"For believing in me enough to risk everything."

"Well, thanks, but, they're still going to kill us." He couldn't push his thoughts past the idea of getting caught.

"They won't find us."

"How do you know that?" he asked.

She sighed and then leaned back in her seat, staring forward. She peeked at the rear view mirror and into the eyes of the man driving. The driver was watching the road. "What's your name?" she called to him.

"I don't have one. And from what I understand, neither do you," he responded dryly.

Deidra smiled and then turned back to Edward. "My father was in the CIA."

Edward's eyes widened with interest.

"He spent a lot of time in South America in the 80s. I was in elementary school when he started hinting to me about what he was doing there. He was gone so much. I asked a lot of questions. I think he was an operative in some drug smuggling thing. Anyway, until he told me, I thought he was just a business man down there. He visited us when we lived in California and told me that he wanted me to learn how to recognize the truth in life. You know, just how to see it in everyday situations. So he taught me to be strong and to prepare for real life." She looked at him and smiled. "I don't think he trusted all the people he worked for. I think he saw some things that changed him. He wanted to be home with us more than he was, but he just couldn't be there."

Edward thought about what it would be like to have a father like hers growing up, having to miss out on the lives of his children because he had to. "Is that why he's helping us?"

"Yes. He knows people that are for the cause—rebels that serve their country faithfully, but know how much it has changed. They are patriots, but they have been burned by the system." She looked down at her lap for a moment and twisted a ring on her finger nervously. "He didn't ask me any details, but he knows that I am on the same path as him in seeking out the truth. I told him that we may have found a piece of the bigger picture and he understood."

Edward didn't want her to suffer disappointment. Even with their lives now on the line, he hoped that whatever it was that she thought she had discovered inside the arm was worth all of this mess they were now stuck in. Personally, he was afraid that she was wrong. It was likely just a tumor. But something in her eyes had convinced him to go with her on the journey instead of running deep into the Nevada mountains.

∂∘⚮

Forty minutes passed as they both studied the desert through their windows. The car turned onto a small road that led them through a series of large rocks in the sand-like dirt. The car continued on as a collection of mountains occupied their view.

Five more minutes went by before they spotted an RV surrounded by a set of large boulders. The car stopped several yards away from it and the driver shut off the engine. A man in a white shirt appeared from the RV and stepped out and into the dirt below. He watched the car for movement and waited.

"This is it," the driver told them. "I can't wait here."

"Okay," Deidra answered. "Come on, Eddie. Let's go."

He looked at her, waiting for her to open the door first. As she pulled the door's handle, she picked up the bag at her feet and proceeded to exit the car. Edward got out slowly and moved around the back of the car to follow her lead. "Are you going to talk to him?"

She looked at the man her father told her was their contact. His hair hung long and loose. A mild desert wind kicked it up and tossed locks of it into his face. The glow that came through the windows of the RV behind him cast a silhouette that was muscular. Deidra took a few steps forward and glanced back at Edward for encouragement.

He forced a fractured smile her way as the car behind them backed up, turned and left. He remembered that they had nothing left to lose and joined her at her side. They walked together to meet the man her father sent them to see.

Deidra spoke first, "Hello. My father told me to come here. My name is Deidra."

"Yes," the tall man answered back. "Your father contacted me. He said you needed a place to go."

"I hope we're not bothering you too much, sir," she added.

"Are you being followed?" he asked.

"Most likely," she admitted. "We have something somebody wants."

"Who is the somebody?"

"Well, it's probably more like a group of somebodies."

"Come inside." The man turned and opened the door to his home and let them in. The walls were covered in smooth southwestern decor that included pictures of family. The lighting was low and the smell of beans came from a small portable stovetop that was on top of his tiny kitchen counter. Edward and Deidra both sat on a bed that had been made to look like a couch covered with decorative pillows. Deidra placed the duffle bag across her lap and noticed that the leak was getting worse. The man took a seat across from them on a small chair and studied them sternly.

"I do not know what you have in the bag, but I want you to take care not to get blood on my things," he warned.

Deidra smiled uncomfortably. "Yes, we have a problem with this thing. We need to, um … do some cutting into it for extraction purposes and then find a place to go where we'll be safe."

"Does it belong to the government?" he asked.

"No. Actually, I don't know. It's hard to tell," she began. "We're not sure who it belongs to but it has something to do with something very serious or it wouldn't be here with us."

The man's face hardened as he leaned back in his seat.

"Anyway, we just need a place to do the surgical stuff." She swallowed hard and waited for the man to react.

His face remained steady, eyeing her carefully, and then he looked at the bag on her lap. "This place is all I have."

"We appreciate your kindness in letting us come here like this. Would it be okay to use your sink?"

"You should do it outside," he demanded.

"No, actually, we can't do that." Deidra was frustrated and became more impatient as the conversation went on. "Listen, I know my father didn't explain much to you about this, but that was because I could only tell him so much over the phone. We don't have a lot of time. I honestly don't know what we have in this bag, but I can tell you that when we cut this man's arm off, something inside it moved under the skin."

Sam crossed his arms and leaned forward, expecting for her to continue.

"I understand my father probably threw this on you unexpectedly and that you aren't too happy that we are here, a couple of strangers, in your home carrying a body part but ...," tears welled up in her eyes as she took a moment to gather her thoughts. She sighed painfully. "We just have to get something out of this arm. I'm telling you, it's something important because a company man was after it."

Sam let his mind sit on the information he had been given. His thoughts raced and he looked around the RV, still wearing the same hardened expression. "You are welcome to use my sink."

Edward and Deidra looked at each other, relieved at the opportunity to move on to the next step on their quest. The dreaded surgery on the arm.

"Thank you, sir," Edward added. It didn't seem appropriate due to the circumstances they were in, but it was all he could think of to say.

"Just clean up when you are finished," said Sam.

Deidra looked at Edward as he shrugged his shoulders and stood to get closer to the sink across from them. Deidra could see pieces of dried up food remnants stuck to its sides and a dried up blue sponge. She extended a hand toward Sam and smiled. "Thanks."

Sam accepted the handshake and smiled in return. "Hurry."

25

"They have taken the arm, Franklin!" the man on the other end of the line yelled. "They have stolen it! The races are finished! That bitch you have helping him isn't helping at all! She's fucking things up!"

Franklin listened in shock. His teeth clenched hard at the angry tone in the man's voice. It was one of his biggest investors. Making any investor angry would have made him nervous enough, but making this investor angry was slightly more dangerous. This investor was connected with the Italian mafia, by rumor. Highly credible rumors.

"Please calm down and explain to me what is going on. I don't see how they would have deviated from the instructions unless something has gone wrong," Franklin explained.

"Frank! Something *has* gone wrong! A federal agent was found dead in our target's hotel room! The arm was taken off the target and not delivered to the location we instructed! This is going to cost us millions! They will come after us for this. It was handed down to us to hand down to you! And who the fuck is this guy in charge of the job?"

Franklin sighed in fear. He didn't believe that Deidra would cross him. There was nothing but loyalty in her eyes. She was committed to the cause behind the races. It was greater to them than others knew. It served an inter-planetary mission integral to alien-human relations. It was the grail of secret research. It was beyond most human comprehension. They were liberating the planet together—rescuing humanity. Franklin viewed himself as a savior. One day in the future, the concept of death would never be the same.

"I don't understand," he murmured. "No one has told me what this is all about. If I knew the details of this assignment, maybe I could help locate them," he said as he lowered his eyes to the floor knowing that he must have made a lapse in judgment. The weakness he loathed in others, was the weakness that allowed him to choose Edward. He was the closest thing he had to a son in this disappointing world. "I have obviously made a mistake and I am ready to fix it. I just need to know what this is about."

"It's about the end of the races! The greys will either take them from us or end them all together! You have everything at stake here, Frank!" the man screamed into the phone frantically. "If you think you can find them, do it NOW!"

The call ended. Franklin sat alone in a large, candlelit room lined with Persian rugs. He sat, tapping the arm of the armchair Deidra had picked out in Paris. It wasn't one he had particularly liked, but it caught her eye unexpectedly and made her screech at the sight of it. After explaining that she wasn't leaving France without it, he gave in.

He thought about what his contact had said to him. He didn't understand how important the job was to keeping the races alive. He didn't know who the target was or why the arm had been detached. He just knew that if the mafia bosses were this panicked about how it was being taken care of, there had to be something seriously wrong.

The mob first contacted Franklin back when the races began. He needed help with funding and they were eager to get involved as potential investors, with interest. He was happy to have them on board. They came across to him as a kinder, more lenient group than the feds had been as business partners in the past. Franklin had always favored dealing with underworld investors anyway. They were more on the level and if they were going to kill you, they would be more likely to look you in the face first before doing it. The feds would just shoot you in the back and tell the media that you were a suicidal cross-dresser.

Franklin reached in front of him to pull open the top drawer of his desk. He grabbed for the gun inside. Funding for his research was now at stake. He needed to prepare a jet for a quick flight to Vegas.

26

"Don't squish it!" Deidra hissed at the back of Edward's head.

He carefully used both hands to guide the arm up from its resting place in the bag on the floor and into the sink they had lined with trash bags. The arm was soaking wet with blood and the only thing protecting Edward's hands were two rubber gloves that would normally be seen in a medical office. Sam offered them to him earlier as they laid newspapers out across the floor near the sink. He didn't ask why Sam had the box of gloves in the first place but had an idea why. Either way, Edward was grateful to have them on at that moment.

As he placed the lifeless arm into the tiny sink, Deidra reached for the surgical tools she had stored in her handbag sitting on the countertop. She unwrapped the tools and removed a scalpel, grasping it firmly between her fingers. Edward held out his hand and looked at her bravely.

"You want to do it?" she asked in surprise.

"Of course I don't but you removed it, so I guess I should open it," he said with a hard swallow.

"I can do it," Sam offered from behind them. He was standing so that he could see over their shoulders. Because he was much taller than they were, he had a pretty good view of the procedure that was about to happen in his sink. He seemed to be excited about the whole thing.

"Oh," Edward began uncomfortably. "That's okay. I can handle it."

Edward did the best he could to pretend that he could get himself through the act of an amateur surgery. He tried his best to remember that the procedure itself couldn't possibly go wrong since it was really more of an extraction than anything else. It was still far from the high school frog dissection he had skipped class to avoid.

"Go ahead, just get started," Deidra encouraged him.

"Okay," he agreed, ready to get it over with and behind them.

He placed his gloved right hand on top of the arm to feel for the lump that had caused them so much trouble that night and located it. He was surprised to find that the lump did exist and placed the scalpel into his right hand to start the extraction. He now used his left hand to feel again for the lump so that he could begin, but the lump moved.

"What the hell?" Edward jumped, causing Deidra to flinch and catch her breath.

"What happened?" she asked.

"It moved!" His eyes were wide and filled with terror. He started to step back but then stopped himself. He wanted to get it over with. They had time against them. "I'm going to grab it and just cut it out of there as fast as I can."

"That's right, Eddie. You can do this." She assured him.

He reached for the arm and stared at the lump. He could see a vibrating motion coming from it. Both hands ready, he brought himself in closer to it, hovering over the sink. He grabbed the lump between his fingers and pinched it as hard as he could handle without vomiting in the process. He placed the scalpel near the edge of it and cut as quickly as he could, digging underneath the lump. He could feel it moving from side to side between his fingers. He finished slicing underneath it as fast as he could as Deidra held out her gloved hands, offering to take it from him.

He placed it into her hands quickly and started breathing again. He felt light headed. "Oh my God," was all he could say at the sight of it.

Deidra held on to it with her hands closed and looked at Edward and Sam for any suggestions.

"Let's put it on a towel so we can look at it," Sam suggested.

"Okay," she agreed. "I'm just making sure it's stopped moving first."

Edward looked around him for a towel and then to Sam. Sam had one ready and threw it to Edward. Edward laid it out on the countertop and then motioned for Deidra to place the thing in her hand onto the towel whenever she was ready.

"I thought when you said it was moving, that you were just saying that," Edward admitted.

"Really?" She asked. "You thought I just made that up?"

She relaxed her shoulders and let go of some of the tension in her arms. She placed her hands closer to the white kitchen towel set out before her. Sam and Edward gathered in closer, anxious to see what was about to happen. She loosened her grip slowly until she felt confident enough to set the rounded object down onto it. The blood surrounding it was smeared all over her gloves.

The three of them stood in silence, hovering over the strange object until Deidra spoke. "I'm going to clean it off," she began quietly. "Then we can see what it is."

She used an end of the towel it was resting on to wipe it off. It now appeared to be more oval in shape than round and it was about the size of a jelly bean.

"Wow," Sam gasped.

"Yeah," Deidra agreed.

"What?" Edward wondered, feeling left out again.

"It's a biological encasing," she explained. "It's like a protective covering. It's alive. Like skin."

"Yes," Sam joined in. "But it's not one I recognize. You said it moved?"

"Yes!" Deidra remembered excitedly. "When it was in his arm, it wiggled around when I pressed on it."

"It may be something new," Sam suggested.

Edward looked at the scalpel nervously. It was on the edge of the kitchen sink. He looked at Deidra and hoped that what he was about to say was something he wouldn't regret later. "Are we going to cut it open?"

She looked at him with a frown and then at the scalpel. "Yes. But let me do it."

There would be no argument from Edward at that point since he had done all the illegal surgical procedures he had wanted to for quite a while. He picked up the scalpel and held it in his hand, waiting for her to be ready for it.

She took it from him and bent herself carefully over the object. Using the tip of the blade, she poked through the membrane of the soft outer covering and a light amount of clear ooze dripped out and mixed with the blood already on the towel.

Edward shuddered.

She stopped and pried open the rest of it with her fingers. She froze only for a few seconds before picking something up from inside the slimy shell she had just cut through and placed it cautiously on a cleaner part of the towel. It was tiny and black in color.

"What is it?" Edward asked.

"I don't know," she replied.

Deidra was confused. It could have been anything, nothing, or a million different things but it didn't matter at that moment because she didn't know either way. She looked at Sam but all he did was shrug his shoulders.

"That's all it is?" Sam added.

"It's something or it wouldn't have caused us so much trouble," she reminded them. "It looks like an electronic device. It has a small hole in the side," she said while squinting and tilting her head closer to it.

Edward pulled off his gloves and began to fold the ends of the trash bags together inside the sink. "I gotta cover this thing. It smells so bad. Should we put it back in the bag they gave us?"

"Who gave you a bag?" Sam asked dryly.

"The bag we brought this thing in? It was given to us by whoever assigned us this job," he answered.

"You mean the job we ditched," Deidra sighed.

"Yeah, that job."

Sam looked at the bag on the floor with a serious expression on his face. "What was in it?"

Edward looked into the air to think before answering. "Well...it had a piece of paper, some cutting wire, and some cable thing."

"What cable thing?" Deidra jumped to attention.

"I don't know. It's in this side pocket." He reached down into the bag and unzipped a pocket on the inside. He pulled out a black cord and held it out for them to see. One end of the cord had a very small connector and the other looked more familiar to him. The cord was only about four inches in length. "Oh ... this part is like the part that my mouse uses on my laptop."

Deidra quickly snatched it from his hands. "Oh my God! This part fits into this thing!"

Sam smiled. "I hope it's waterproof."

"Sam!" Deidra said excitedly. "Do you have a computer we can use?"

Sam's face suddenly filled with concern. "That is a lot to ask. I am sorry. It seems too dangerous."

Deidra's heart sank. "Please? Offline, they will never know! We will get out of here right away afterwards. It could change history! Don't you want to see what it is? You know they are hiding something good!" she begged.

"We will buy you a new computer. We don't have a lot of time," Edward reminded him.

"I will find us another driver to get us out of here as soon as we are done. A safe one. Verified. We can pay you a very large sum of money. We can transfer it into the account of your choice or deliver it in cash to the location of your choice." Deidra waited for his response.

"I don't know what that thing will do once it is plugged in. You have to take this computer with you and wipe it clean," Sam informed them.

"Okay," she held out her hand to shake his but then stopped herself. She quickly pulled the plastic gloves off of her hands, remembering how much blood was on them. She grabbed a paper towel from a roll seated on the windowsill in front of her to wipe the cable clean of the blood it may have come into contact with. When the device was clean enough, she shook Sam's hand. "Thanks, friend."

Sam then pulled his laptop out from under his bed, opened it, and set it on top of the counter next to the small black device she was plugging one end of the cable into. The computer came to life showing a wallpaper display of wild flowers. The flowers glowed before them in the darkened room.

She hesitated before plugging the USB connector part of the cable into the side of the computer. "Okay. Let's hope this thing doesn't kick anything on that can track us."

"Cheers to that," Edward scoffed. He took his place behind Deidra at the counter, ready to see what would happen on the computer from over her left shoulder. Sam did the same, ready to watch over her on the other side.

She plugged in the cable and they waited in silence as the computer worked to recognize the device.

Deidra held her breath as she used the touch pad to activate the menu to find a drive letter for the device.

"That's it!" Sam said.

"Drive 'F'?"

"Yes! Click on it!"

"It's reading it like a regular USB drive," she said, barely able to control her breathing. "Fuck," she gasped. "It's a video file."

Edward tensed up, preparing himself for what was to come. The video player loaded and darkness took over the screen. Video control buttons loaded and appeared at the bottom of the screen and instead of a regular video title, numbers showed up in their place.

"Recognize it?" Deidra asked, obviously speaking to Sam.

"Yes," he replied. "It's older. Maybe 1980s. It looks like it's Air Force."

She let the pointer hover over the play button for a second and then clicked it. She quickly adjusted the volume as it began, but there was no sound to be heard when the video started.

Inside a small room without windows, fluorescent lights from above illuminated a bare concrete floor. The room was empty for only seconds before a group of people entered. It looked like a family. There was a boy, about ten years old that entered first, looking behind him for the next person, a woman, to follow. A man and a teenage boy entered seconds later and all of them stood, looking around frantically and then seemed to look straight into the camera. There was a mirrored window concealing the camera that was filming them, but they must have known it. A small girl entered last. The father reached forward quickly and clutched her in his arms. She looked about 6 years old.

Seconds passed before a man in a beret entered. It seemed that he was standing there speaking to them as they all stared at him, but only the back of his head and a small part of his collar was visible. It was easy to tell that it was a military collar that he wore. The father looked angry at the man in the beret and started to yell but the video was silent. The grainy, faded-looking video glitched for a moment, but then continued on with the father yelling and the children cowering with the mother.

The military man abruptly left them. In the frame, the top corner of a door could be seen opening and closing as the military man exited. The family huddled together, the children looking around in terror. Six long seconds went by before the door reopened and four small figures were pushed into the room. The two smaller children began to cry and the mother buried her head into the back of her husband's shoulder. The four greys stood in front of the humans facing the military men that followed them in. There were now three military men and they seemed to be in a confrontation with the aliens. One of the men pushed one of the greys down onto the floor in front of the teen boy. The boy instinctively reached over to help him, as the alien seemed to be in pain.

The military men then did something as they stepped back and further out of frame that sent the humans into a frenzied panic. The greys outstretched their arms as if to beg, and one moved quickly to cover the small human girl behind him with its body.

The tips of weapons could then be seen in frame, and the humans clutched one another as the greys flailed their arms in the air and opened their mouths in horror before they all fell, in contorted movements, limp to the ground, as shot after shot was fired.

The grey that had done its best to protect the small child had fallen with its hand against her sandy hair. The human father was lifeless with his arm around her waist.

The tips of the guns dropped out of frame and only the soldiers' berets could be seen as they exited the room. Blood had been splattered against the white walls and the screams must have been unbearable to hear. As the last man left, he quickly glanced back into the camera behind the two-way mirror, stepped over the teen boy's arm, and exited.

27

When Edward noticed that Deidra was no longer standing in front of him at the computer's controls, he looked back to see her seated on the bed-couch behind them. Her hands covered her mouth.

"Turn it off," she groaned.

"It ended," he tried to assure her.

"No!" she yelled. "Unplug it from the computer! Take it out!"

Sam knelt to the floor next to her and touched her knee. She flinched slightly, but still sat frozen with her eyes wide in disbelief. She looked him in the eyes in a state of shock.

"I know that was hard to watch," Sam told her. "It was awful. They are in a better place now. You have to believe that. I know your father would be proud of you for intercepting this before it disappeared forever. You can change the world with this, Deidra. I know you can make good come from this."

"It was Franklin," she buried her face into her hands and began to sob.

"What?" Edward stepped in closer to try to understand her through the tears.

"It was Franklin! He killed them! It was him!"

Edward stood and waited for the words to register in his head correctly. She was convinced it was him. He wanted to play the video back to see for himself. He needed to be as sure as she was. "Can we see a still shot of the last guy in the video?" he asked Sam.

Sam looked at Deidra for an objection, but she was too distraught to react. He got up and used the touchpad to search the ending of the video until he found the correct spot. He then let it hang there for Edward to see.

Edward reluctantly moved in closer to the computer, knowing in the back of his head that she had to be right about it because she was right about everything. Then he saw it for himself. It was Franklin, about thirty years younger, looking straight into the camera.

"We have to go, Eddie," Deidra said while wiping away tears. "I'm going to get our driver back or find another one right now."

"No," Sam told them. "Relax. I will find you one myself."

28

Franklin waited as the private jet was being prepared to take him to Las Vegas. His men had to be on their trail. If they weren't, they would be very soon. By the time he arrived, both of them would be his to question and whatever the assignment was that they were fucking up would be set straight again.

His cell phone rang.

"Hello?"

"Have your men found them?" The raspy voice on the other end asked.

"I don't know yet. I'm going to be over there soon enough to help search for them myself."

"Collin Bennett is gone," the man informed him.

Franklin sighed. "Well, that was to be expected, I guess."

"What the hell do you plan on doing over there anyway, Mr. Andrews?" the man yelled into the phone.

"Sir, I plan to clean up my own mess. I would like you to call off your men and let me handle it from this point."

"Mr. Andrews! By now, the people you entrusted with this job have enough evidence to ruin everything we have built!" The man coughed into the phone. "How can you repair that?"

"I plan on putting them down and getting it back. Whatever it is, I will get it back and take it to whatever location you ask me to ... personally." Franklin responded while closing his eyes, horrified at the thought of killing them, but understanding it as a necessity.

"Well, let me help to put a fire under your shoes, Mr. Andrews," the man said with a sharpened tongue. "The thing you will be returning to us is a small, black device with a video loaded onto it. It was implanted into the arm of a teacher by a rogue group of aliens that want to destroy our drag races! They want to stop the exploitation of humans used and killed in races for profit! Can you believe that shit? A human rights group run by alien shitheads!" The man now laughed hysterically. "The video was on its way to a science fiction convention in Las Vegas in the arm of that teacher. Our federal contacts intercepted an email this guy made to some Ph.D. that was speaking at the event. He was going to have him help remove it and analyze it. If they had succeeded, they would have gone into fucking shock watching a nice little family being gunned down along with some greys they had tried to help when their ship crashed on our planet in the fucking woods while this family was on a camping trip! You know what I mean, Frank? Do you know what I fucking mean?"

Franklin's body was numb. Every limb shook and went limp. The phone slipped from his hand but he caught it midair and quickly placed it back to his ear. His hands were shaking.

"Did you hear me, Franklin?" the man growled. "The greys won't like that video will they? I heard you look like shit in it."

"Stop!" he yelled back. "Even if we get it back, how can we stop them from trying to get another one out there? What group is it? How do you know what happened anyway?"

"The greys hate these rebel groups. It probably took too much effort for them to get the video in the first place. Our government knows not to deal with them. They get in the way of their DNA research. I don't know if we can stop them again, but we need to stop them this time. The next race the greys are holding will debut the products from our DNA labs. That's a lot of money. Once they are hooked on that stuff, they won't care what happened back in 19-fuckin'-82. We can't take this thing to other planets if it gets shut down on Earth!"

"They won't invest if they see that video," Franklin agreed robotically.

"That's right. But if we can get one more week to keep it from them, the deal will be done and our race will be an instant universal success. You know how money hungry these bastards are. If we don't get a chance to prove it to them though—that we have the best races in the universe—it's over." The man cleared his throat. "This is bad karma, Frank. This is that shit they hate—dirty deaths."

"Yes," Franklin agreed. "Dirty."

"You don't want them to get that video, do you? You have a connection with them, don't you?"

"They see it like I do," Franklin told him nostalgically. "They see the art in it. They see how the life behind the driver is the greater picture. That life is emotion and pain. It's pain."

"That's right, Frank," the raspy-voiced man's words softened. "And they can't get a crop like ours on any other planet. They need us. They need this race and our products—our racers. It brings them joy to see the win, or the death. Clean deaths. They feel it happen ... like addicts."

"They do feel it." Franklin's eyes swelled and tears fell down his face. "I'll stop them. I'll get the video back. With every part of me, I will stop them."

He ended the call and watched as his pilot motioned to him from the entrance of the plane that it was ready to go.

It's for art.

29

"Did I ever tell you the story about that time I did a taco run with Crazy Miguel?" Edward asked Deidra as she paced the tiny area between the bed and the bathroom.

She stopped to look at him in disgust and then continued her nervous energy back and forth again. Sam was still crammed in the bathroom speaking on the phone to some secret contact and had requested that they be as quiet as possible while he did his best to secure them a ride back to Vegas.

"It's a funny story," Edward told her.

"Now? Really?"

"Why not?" he asked in all seriousness.

"Go ahead then." She shrugged her shoulders and put her hands in the air.

Edward adjusted his feet so that he was comfortable enough to tell her the story. He was confident that she would appreciate it once she heard it and felt giddy inside just thinking about it. "Okay, you're going to love this!"

"Fuck, just tell me!"

"Okay, you know how you were complaining to Franklin about how you thought working with me was like having a sharpened fork scratching your skin repeatedly?"

Deidra rolled her eyes at him. "Yes, Eddie. But that was because you interrupted me while I was roughing up the chief that day. You couldn't just keep your mouth shut and let me threaten him on my own. You go and knock a picture of his family off the wall for no damn reason! 'You better pay us or next time it will be them!' You made me look stupid!"

"I was trying to intimidate him," he explained while nodding his head and raising his eyebrows knowingly.

"Oh my God, Eddie," she laughed. "It was the chief of police."

"Okay, well after that you told Franklin that you wanted to work alone again on collections."

"Duh."

"So, then he said to you that you needed to find a way to get along with me or he would pair you up with Miguel again," Edward reminded her.

"Oh yeah," she chuckled so hard she bent over and almost fell to the floor. "Shhh! Stop making me laugh!"

"… because 'you can't do collections alone,' he said."

"That's right! You said it just like him," she laughed.

"Then you were like, 'Oh my Gawd! Not Crazy Miguel! Okay, I will work with stupid Edward!'" He imitated her voice in a way that would make her laugh even harder than before.

"Stop it, Eddie," she insisted while doing her best to suppress her laughter. "Sam's trying to help us."

"Yeah, it's okay," he collected his thoughts and looked toward the bathroom before continuing. "So, I met Miguel a few days afterward."

"Really? Ewwww. Why?"

"Because I was asked to go with him to get some food for a meeting Franklin was setting up at his office downtown."

"Oh," she smiled and took a seat next to him on the bed. "So who did he kill in the process?"

Edward sat back a little, smiled, and then proceeded to tell her the story.

❧❦

"Hey there, Buddy! You must be Ed," Miguel said in a chipper tone.

Miguel wasn't a bad guy. Edward knew it. He knew this because if Deidra had a problem with him, he had to be fine. What Edward saw walking through the foyer of Franklin's office building was a well-dressed, mild-mannered gentleman with an eloquent walk. It was very much like a strut. Not the kind that would lead one to think of him as obnoxious or cocky, but one that was reminiscent of European royalty. Slow and confident—in no hurry to prove anything to anybody. A strut of birthright.

"Edward. I prefer Edward," he said while holding out his hand. "Nice to meet you, Miguel."

"Hey! How did you know my name?" Miguel laughed. "Just kidding, Edward. I'm sure they told you about me."

Miguel was a little person. He was easy to describe amongst the rest of Franklin's crew, but Edward hadn't been informed about his size at all. He had only been told that he should be careful not to upset him. He was short, but had a handsome face and a very neatly shaven goatee. His hair was thick and dark, but speckled with some grays here and there.

"No, actually, they just said that a guy named Miguel would be taking me on an errand with him. Nothing else. Really," he answered uncomfortably.

"No problem, Edward," he smiled. "So I guess we need to stop and get some food for these bums, huh? They get pretty cranky if they don't have something to eat during these big meetings of theirs. How about some tacos? Oh … and some cupcakes." Miguel winked. "They probably want those, too."

"I think that sounds great."

They arrived in a timely manner in front of Jimmy's Taco Town. It seemed like a good enough place. The exterior was painted bright green and pleasantly decorated with a variety of oversized potted cacti. With an hour to kill before the meeting, they might have time to have a few tacos themselves. Since tacos are a food group in Texas, Edward didn't want to neglect that fact.

"... and so I dropped out of Harvard as soon as I realized that its purpose had become, over time, meaningless to me," Miguel explained to him as they walked through the door at Jimmy's.

"Wow! Really?"

"Yeah. It just wasn't the place for me any longer. My political and ethical views had taken a beating after some philosophy classes back home. I thought that I would find myself again in law, but it turned out that I felt ... lost instead." Miguel looked up in a gaze. Reflective, with a hint of concern. "But enough about me. Let's place that order. Muchos tacos await us!"

Edward stared at the large wooden menu situated above the cash register area. The guy behind the counter smiled patiently and waited for them in silence.

Miguel rapped his fingers on the laminate countertop and frowned. It wasn't an angry frown. It was a frown of contemplation. Tacos took deep thought. With so many varieties, the decisions were exponentially endless. "So what do you think? Half of them chicken and the other half beef?"

"Sure, why not? And a few for us, too, right?"

"Of course, Amigo!"

Then Edward saw it—a green, blurry reflection. It glowed in a large decorative mirror behind the man in the Jimmy's cap waiting to take their order. It was the blur of a green pompadour. It was being combed and admired in the glass of the restaurant's door. And then, that dirty, skinny, lanky Elvis-wannabe noticed him. And then it smirked. Johnny Feinstein was now entering the building.

"Shit," Edward whispered. He tensed up and clenched his teeth together.

Miguel was oblivious to the ungodly presence of Feinstein. He didn't smell the years of cigarette smoke emitting from Johnny's leather jacket, or the toxic scent that tons of cheap hairspray layered on his head gave out. He didn't notice the sounds that came from Johnny's combat boots as they stomped clumsily on the floor behind them. And he didn't seem to notice Edward snarl as Johnny slapped him on the back, forcefully pushing Edward into the counter.

"Watch out, you damn fucks!" Johnny said to them with a hiss. He squeezed his way between the two of them and looked over the menu, knowing full well that he had every last part of it memorized. He bumped them at the hips with his own to push them further away from his new spot at the counter.

The man in the Jimmy's cap looked confused.

"Excuse me, sir," Miguel said to Johnny with a friendly tone. "We were about to place our order. Can you back up a little until it's your turn?"

"Well, I'm sorry but I don't think kids are allowed to order without their mommy, little guy!" Johnny snickered. "Go play outside with your pussy friend for a while until I'm done!"

The man behind the counter backed up a little, his smile unaffected.

Miguel looked at Edward, finally noticing that he was about as pumped up as a prize fighter about to enter the ring. Or like a cat about to pounce. One of the two.

"Hey, dammit!" Edward yelled with his fists clenched. It didn't come out of him the way it should have, but at least his voice didn't crack in the process. "We were here first and we are placing our order! Why don't *you* wait outside?"

Johnny looked at Edward and then at the man in the Jimmy's hat. "Did this stupid fucker just say something to me?"

The two cooks in the back were now gathering up front to stand behind the cashier for a better view.

"Yes. I did say something to you!" Edward yelled. "And if you don't step back and give us our space to order, I will be forced to ask you to leave!"

The two patrons that had been sitting at a small table nearby crouched down while running out the front door. They made sure to take their tacos and drinks with them. Johnny slammed a hand down on the counter and faced Edward. "*You* will ask me to leave? That's really nice of you, jerk-fuck. I love your manners. You remind me of my sister...OOOOUCH! WHAT THE FUCK?!" Johnny screamed at the top of his lungs.

He spun around and looked down at Miguel. Edward could see a knife lodged into the back of Johnny's thigh. The two men standing behind the cashier ducked down behind the counter. The cashier just stood with his mouth gaping as Johnny proceeded to reach for Miguel's neck with both hands.

"Get off him!" Edward screamed. He repeatedly slammed his fists into Johnny's back.

Miguel then, while in a choke hold, reached down into his sock and pulled out another blade. A second later it, too, was stuck in Johnny Feinstein. This time, it was in his side.

"Jesus, Miguel!" Edward cried out.

Johnny let go of Miguel's throat and pulled the knife out of his side.

"Let's go!" Edward begged.

Miguel kicked Johnny repeatedly in the shins until he fell to the ground. "When I want fucking tacos, I want my fucking tacos!"

Edward ran back and forth with no idea which direction to take. He kept going toward the door but would then stop and run back toward Miguel and see Johnny wincing in pain before running back to the door again. There was blood all over the floor. "We have to go!"

Miguel stood up straight and brushed off his shirt with his hands. "Edward! You hold this guy down! You," he pointed at a cook that had snuck back into the kitchen, "make me a dozen chicken fajita tacos and a dozen beef fajita tacos! NOW!"

"S-s-si, señor," the cook replied.

❧

"I got a driver," Sam interrupted. "She should be here in thirty minutes."

"Thanks," Deidra said. She then turned back to Edward and tilted her head.

"What?" he asked.

"So you held down Johnny for him?"

"Yes. He was pretty messed up though. It's not like it was a hard thing to do," he reminded her. He knew that he didn't have to pretend to be a tough guy around her. She had already seen him at his weakest several times. "He was slipping in his own blood each time he tried to get up."

"You held down Johnny Feinstein?" She asked again, this time with emphasis on his first and last names.

"Yes."

"Eddie," Deidra leaned toward him, "Johnny was taken out that night after the race. Franklin had him killed."

Sam seemed to become interested in the conversation and leaned against the kitchen counter to listen after he checked to make sure that there wasn't any blood there first that might stain his white shirt.

"But he was there," Edward insisted. "It was him."

"I believe you. I'm just kind of surprised, that's all."

"Well, obviously Franklin didn't have him killed. He got away," Edward suggested. "Don't you even want to know what happened after I held him down?"

"I do," Sam answered.

"You guys got the tacos and brought them to the meeting," she began. "Miguel put Johnny in the trunk of Johnny's car after hog-tying him and taping his mouth shut with rope and tape he had with him because he is a scary, scary man that has stuff like that with him at all times and I don't suggest that you hang out with him again for that reason and many others that I am not allowed to tell you about and the tacos were great because I ate one at the meeting," Deidra said in one long breath. "The cupcakes were good, too."

"Oh," Edward replied.

"But Johnny was killed that night of the race," she said. "We helped get rid of his body."

"We?"

"On the way to Franklin's house that night. Remember? We stopped at a bon fire the mechanics had going."

"On that hill," he started remembering.

"Yes. We stopped there to make sure it had been taken care of."

Edward remembered clearly now. He remembered how the fire highlighted her pale face and dark hair perfectly. He sat in the car with Franklin as she walked toward the blaze and stood next to it. She stared into it. The wind blew the flames in every direction as she turned back to look at them. From where she stood, he could hardly see her eyes but hoped, harder than he had hoped for anything before that moment, that she was looking only at him.

"Do you remember that fire? We use them to destroy any evidence after a race."

"Yes." He looked down from her gaze. He then remembered going to a large mansion and being given food and some ice for his eye. *Jesus, I didn't know that was his house. So that's where they have sex…naked.*

Edward twisted his mouth and raised his eyebrows at her, trying to bring himself back to the topic at hand. "But he was being stabbed and kicked by Miguel."

"Yes. I heard you."

"Then what are you suggesting?" he asked cautiously.

She looked down to break eye contact with him. "We need to finish cleaning up this mess and then pack everything up."

"Deidra," Edward pressed further. "What's going on with Johnny then?"

"Bring the arm, or what's left of it, because we need to get rid of it safely."

She got up and reached for the paper towels in the windowsill and caught Sam's eye watching her.

"Do you have any kind of cleaning products I can use to help get this stuff contained correctly?" she asked. "Bleach, preferably?"

"Yes. Under the sink," he answered, while reaching down to help her find the bleach she had requested. "DNA labs?" he whispered in her ear.

She closed her eyes and nodded yes. "They love our racers."

30

Deidra asked their driver to drop them someplace near a good selection of hotels off the strip. Someplace busy, but not too busy. She wanted a variety of hotels to choose from. Motels were fine also so it would be okay to throw some of those into the mix as well. She handed the driver five thousand dollars through the window before they left Sam's place and made one other request. On the way from Pahrump to Vegas—she wanted her to pull over someplace desolate so they could discard something they had with them that was no longer needed.

When they reached the city, Deidra began to check her phone frequently. Edward tried looking over at the screen but she would turn herself just enough so that he couldn't see. He remembered her telling him recently how important it was to be extra careful on the phone. He knew it could be used to trace people. Seeing her on it only made him wonder if she might have some secret application that could block out anyone spying on them. She was just too cautious to use a cell phone in a situation like this. It didn't seem like her at all.

"Don't worry," she said without looking away from her phone. "I have some secret app that blocks out anyone tracing us. I'm just messing with some settings on it. Are you hungry?"

"Wow. That's weird."

"Huh?"

The driver came to a stop after a slow turn that caught Deidra's attention. "Where are we?" she called out to her.

"Tropicana Avenue. Tons of places to stay. Is this all right with you?" the driver asked.

"Yeah, thanks," Deidra said after taking a second to glance around through the window. She then locked her phone and looked at Edward.

"Are we just getting out here?" he asked.

"Yes. Don't worry," she smiled.

They exited the car in front of a fast food restaurant. Deidra handed the driver another 500 dollars and then motioned for them to wait until the driver pulled away. Deidra then dialed a number and waited for someone to answer while looking all around her. "Yeah, hello?" she said into the phone. "Okay, hold on for just a second. Sorry. What? ...Yes, of course I'm using it. I could die over this. You think I want them to trace us?"

She then looked at Edward.

"What?" he asked.

"Maybe you should go look around for a place to eat."

"We're standing in front of one."

"Look for a different one. Just walk up the street a little and tell me what you see."

"Like fast food?" he asked.

Deidra was beginning to get annoyed. "Yes. Whatever."

He walked up the street a few yards and looked around. There were only more fast food places, a diner, and some gas stations. He looked back to see that she was in a deep kind of a conversation. He knew that she was just looking for a way to keep him busy so that she could discuss her plan on what to do with the device now that she had it. He was thankful that she could contact the right people to help them, but felt left out of the excitement. Had he proven himself to be the specimen of man that he had hoped to be? No, but he needed a chance to take control of a situation first in order to do so. Sending him out for a walk to stare at places to eat wasn't enough. He wanted a real task. He wanted to deal with the secret contacts and the underground street-toughs. Then his phone, that he thought was turned off, rang.

He pulled his phone out of his pants pocket and looked at it. His heart pounded. It was Franklin. "Shit!" He ran back toward Deidra and stopped in front of her just as the phone stopped ringing. She put her hand out in front of him and scrunched up her face.

"Okay, thanks. I will." She then ended the call. "What?!" she asked Edward.

"Franklin is calling me!"

Deidra laughed. "Well, when he calls again, you should answer."

His phone rang again and Edward's eyes bulged. He held the phone out for her to see like a child producing tattletale evidence to his mother.

"Answer it!" she hissed.

Edward pressed the screen of the phone with his index finger and held it up to his ear. "Hello?"

"Where are you?" Franklin asked in a deep growl.

Deidra shook her head as if to tell Edward that it would be a bad idea to tell Franklin, the man that most likely wanted to kill them for screwing up his job, where they were. Edward made a face at her and lipped the word, "duh."

"Look, we are doing what we have to," Edward explained to him with forced confidence.

"You are stealing." Franklin corrected him.

"Listen. This isn't what you think it is. It's turned into something else, so, I'm sorry." Edward was shaking. He waited for Franklin to scream something back at him and tensed his muscles in preparation for it.

"Where is she?" was all he asked.

"Uh," Edward looked at Deidra and she pointed behind him and started to walk down the sidewalk. Edward followed her, unsure where she was leading him. "She's not here."

"Yes she IS!" Franklin yelled in return. "Put her on the damn phone, Eddie!"

"Look, it's not about her," he began. "It's about doing what's right. That's all we're trying to do …"

"You are stupid as fuck, Eddie. Trusting her? You will find out the truth. It pains me to see you doing this. You are feeding into her sickness. She's taking you down with her … into her madness." Franklin paused, listening for a moment to be sure that Edward was still listening to him. "Her father did this to her. He ruined her sanity. This is not what it seems, Eddie. Don't let her do this to you!"

"I saw it." Edward confessed. "I saw it. Don't fuck with me. Stop trying to be my guardian. You are lying!"

"You saw what?!"

"End it," Deidra said. "Now."

"You saw what?" Franklin demanded to know.

He ended the call and looked to Deidra for their next move.

"We are staying here," she pointed.

It was a budget motel that didn't look overly appealing.

"Our room is booked. Let's get in there and get this taken care of," she advised. "We probably need to hurry. And it would be great if you could go across the street to the gas station and get me some gummy bears and a soda."

31

Outside of Steve's apartment, the automatic sprinkler system turned on. It whined a high-pitched, labored sound causing him to smile and sit up straight for a moment to stretch. It was the reminder he very much needed to break himself away from the computer screen that evening. It had been hours since he had stopped for a bathroom break, a drink, or for anything. It was proving to be a busy night though. One he had least expected.

In the middle of doing his regular watch on news headlines and searching the stories that didn't make it to the mainstream press that day, Steve received an unusual phone call. Being on duty that night meant that he was expected to do more than just take the call. He had to make the decision on what to do with the information he received in the call—on his own. It strained his nerves each time it was his turn to be on watch. Nothing ever came to them. Nothing that wasn't merely a cry for help from a victim within the system ever came to them. But this time it did, and this one was different. It was a cry for exposure. It was a cry for justice, that if ignored, would be taken elsewhere immediately. It was the call he needed to prove his worth to the cause. He would do what he could to handle it as quickly and efficiently as possible. The lady on the phone had convinced him of that right away.

He rubbed his eyes and looked at the time. He needed to force himself to pull away just long enough to get a drink of water, but as Steve got up to do so, his cell phone rang. He turned frantically in place to locate the sound. He shuffled papers away next to his keyboard, looking for his cell. "There you are!" he sung before answering the call. "Hello, my man!"

"Hey," the man answered flatly. "What's the big deal?" he asked, not impressed with whatever he had heard on his voice-mail Steve left earlier in the evening.

"I got a message from a source saying to get ready for a release of info."

"How big?" the man yawned.

"Big," Steve proclaimed proudly.

"I need more than that, dude."

"This is legit. I'm supposed to get it in about 10 minutes. I wish you had called back earlier so we could work out the details."

The man on the other end of the call gasped. "What kind of shit comes in like that? You believe everything you hear? You need to watch what you put our mark on, man. What if it's a false alarm? What then? What source?"

"Listen, dude," Steve asked politely and impatiently at the same time. "I wouldn't waste time on something fake. The source is serious, and it's do or die. If we don't take it, it risks being lost. They claim that they will self-produce it if they have to. But, I'm telling you, man. This could really be good for us."

Steve waited for a reaction but there was only some confused breathing over the silence.

"So do you want me to turn it away?" Steve asked, hoping the answer would be 'no'.

"Damn, dude!" the man sighed. Their line of work never seemed to take them down the clear cut path. But no one ever said that being an underground activist would be easy. "I need more info to get some channels of distribution worked out."

"You should come over. All I can tell you is that as soon as I got the call, I produced the intro and got our lines ready. It will be here soon."

The man took a deep breath in and exhaled. "I can be there in a few minutes. Should I stop and get some beer?" he asked.

"Yeah. Definitely."

32

Deidra still could not see Edward in the light she wanted to see him in. He wasn't savvy, cool, or even sinister enough to pull this thing off without her. He hung around with the big dogs, but he was a Chihuahua inside. And if he had been a dog, his dog name would be Princess.

He wasn't a hitman or a real bad guy. He was genuine and soft. The tough-guy attitude he was forcing into his cell at Franklin was transparent. Franklin knew Edward's history better than Edward could have. Their quick conversation reminded her of a father and son dance. Still, she had to remember to praise him for his effort. Deidra made a mental note of it and then returned to stressing out over the situation unfolding around them. It was a situation they couldn't have avoided. Franklin was closing in on them.

To her, it was their destiny. The device had been placed in their care on purpose. It was their manifesto, a chance to open the eyes of the world. To take from the world its innocence, and to push the human state of existence into a new era.

She led them into the lobby of the motel and checked them in. On the way up to their room, she scanned the hallways and listened closely to the sounds coming from each room they passed. She had come to accept her habitually suspicious nature. It was something she once despised about herself, like an obsessive compulsion. Growing to understand this compulsion as a gift had taken time. It was transferred to her by her nurturing father. All he wanted was to protect her from the world he had come to know. A world that was not the honest place filled with candy as children expected it to be.

She unlocked the door to their room and allowed Edward to enter first. He glanced around before taking a step inside, careful to have his hand on the holster of the gun in his jacket while doing so. He wondered for a moment if she had sent him in first just in case they had been set up. She felt some guilt for using him in that way, but there was no such thing as surviving without the use of simple logic.

Truth for her had become a passion greater than anything else she had ever focused on in life. She knew Edward thought of her as delusional. It had to have been a great leap of faith to enable him to believe that she was actually on to something. The trip to Pahrump, if anything, helped him to see that she was on the right track. She remembered his quivering at the site of the arm being unwrapped on Sam's countertop. Then, the guilt she felt for getting Sam even remotely connected to the mess they were in hit her. Her father had saved Sam's life in Cuba and hid him away from the world to keep him out of trouble. Deidra hoped that she and Edward hadn't ruined that for him.

She sat on the edge of the bed and opened the laptop. After it booted up, she quickly logged in to her email. There were some low-level cleaning programs she needed to run. She had little time to decide to run one of them before or after uploading the video to the location she was given. She had programs that supposedly didn't exist saved in her email that could disguise the computer's MAC address or present an alternate IP address if needed. There would be no way for them to know she was online. Edward watched as she set the computer aside and texted on her phone. He had an idea of what she was about to do next.

She looked at him for a minute before speaking. "Why didn't you get anything for yourself to eat?"

Edward looked down at the small plastic bag in his hand. It contained only the items she had requested him to get. "I don't know."

Minutes passed and the computer started to show the icons of the programs she had loaded onto it. She moved quickly to click them open and mess with their settings. She needed to finish loading them so that she could get to work. She pulled the device out of her handbag and set it and its special cable beside her.

"Maybe you should take a nap," she suggested to him.

"I probably should, but I don't know how I will be able to sleep."

She looked at his heavy eyes and studied the bags that had collected under them. He sat on a chair, slouched into an awkward position. The room smelled like mold and the traffic outside was noisy. "At least lay down on the bed for a while until I get this thing sent. We all need to rest sometimes. The brain needs it."

He took her offer and was careful not to bump her or the computer while he was next to her. He curled up into a ball close to the pillows and closed his eyes. He placed the bag of gummy bears and the soda next to her, just close enough for her to feel them there, and he began to snore almost instantly.

There was a muffled sound outside the door. Edward shot up from the bed and looked around him. Deidra wasn't there. The computer was folded closed on the desk against the wall. He remained still and listened for her in the bathroom.

The voices got closer to the door. He could hear her. She was trying to keep the man calm, but his angry voice kept interrupting her. The door opened, and she walked in with Franklin's gun to her back. He shut the door behind them and bolted it.

"Wake the fuck up, Eddie," Franklin said. He jammed the gun into her back, pushing her further into the room. "I want you to be wide awake while I kill her."

"Jesus," Edward mumbled in shock as he tried to set himself straight. He ran his fingers through his hair and went to adjust his jacket before Franklin stopped him.

"Wait, Eddie," Franklin insisted. "Don't you have a gun in that jacket?"

Edward looked down at himself and then remembered. "Yes. I do."

"Well, take it out and join the party!" Franklin smiled.

Edward looked at Deidra for guidance but she only shook her head and looked down.

"Come on, Eddie. This is going to be fun," Franklin joked.

"Stop calling me 'Eddie,'" he said while taking his gun out slowly and setting it on the bed in front of him.

"No, no, no," Franklin began. "Put the gun back in your hand and get ready to use it."

"Why?"

"Because I'm going to shoot her and then you will be angry about it and shoot me afterward. That's how it works." Franklin ran his fingers down the back of Deidra's hair and she shivered.

"Leave her alone!" Edward yelled in her defense. "What the fuck is going on? It's over, Franklin! She sent the video out. It's probably all over the Internet by now!" he yelled.

"Oh, I know it is," Franklin assured him. "I saw it!"

Edward placed his hand over the gun with caution, not sure how serious Franklin was about allowing him to actually use it. He watched Franklin's facial expression as he placed a good grip on it and pointed it at him loosely.

"I saw it on the way over. I had people watching you two and they saw you buying gummy bears at the store and followed you back. That's cute. Deidra's favorite horrible candy. Fucking gummy bears! I hate those fucking little fuckers!" Franklin spat as he yelled.

"You are loud," Deidra said softly, her eyes still focused on the ground.

"What the fuck is wrong with her?" Franklin asked. "Has she been drinking?"

"What do you care?" Edward asked.

"I want her to pay full attention to what I have to say to her," Franklin said as he placed the gun to her temple and his mouth to her ear, "as I fuck up HER PASSING!"

Edward sat closer to the edge of the bed and tried to gain a better grip on the handle of his gun. He knew this was the time to act tough. If there was ever a time to psych himself into it, this would be it. "What the hell are you talking about?"

"Oh, come on!" Franklin laughed into the air. "She didn't ramble on and on about it to you? Don't play stupid, Eddie!"

"I can assure you that I'm not playing. I really don't know what you mean!" Edward began to notice Deidra swaying slightly.

"Well, since she fucked up MY PASSING, I am going to fuck up HERS. I worked years and years to get that stint in the Air Force off my psychic record. Now this," Franklin sighed. He placed the gun more firmly against her head. "Now, I have this scar to go out with. It stays with you. The trauma stays. I don't have enough time to make up for it now. I just don't have the strength to hide it from them any longer. I have to take it with me. And now, she has to go out like this. In a dirty little motel room."

Edward thought about it for a moment and tried to understand. "Are you talking about … karma?"

"Yes. Residual energy. She ruined my name on Earth." He pushed the gun harder to her skin. "Didn't you?"

"Stop," she said, slurring and looking at Edward in fear. "Shoot him. Don't worry about me."

"Yes, Eddie," Franklin agreed. "You should shoot me. I want you to. Did you have fun uploading that video, Deidra?

Did it win you any points with the underground somehow? Did they pay you?"

"No," she yelled. "They didn't pay me! It was for the truth! You didn't work that evil off. You killed innocent people! Those weren't criminals or lowlifes ... they were children and ... you hid it from our investors! You should have told the greys and asked them to help you!"

"I was doing MY JOB!" Franklin screamed into her ear. He shook violently and grabbed her arm tight, still holding the gun to her head.

Edward was going numb inside and held the gun up to point it at Franklin.

"Go ahead, Eddie," he said. "I'm going to kill her. You need to shoot me."

Edward cringed and tears welled up in his eyes. He looked to Deidra and saw that she was crying. Silently and uncontrollably, she was crying. The tears rolled down her face. Edward corrected his posture. "Just tell me something."

"What," Franklin asked.

"Why do you have to kill her also?"

Franklin paused to blink a few times before explaining. "Because she has worked on and prepared for her passing for years. I'm not giving that to her. She took mine. And I paid for it, too. Everything she has now is because of me."

"What do you mean?"

"Her education, her connections, her abilities to communicate with them ... everything. I paid for her masters and was paying for her doctorate in parapsychology. Technically, she's one of the only true parapsychologists in the world. She has more knowledge on the supernatural than any human on Earth!" Franklin said with anger. "But that's because I paid for it, supported her, found the right people to create a program for her— just for her! I got her involved in The Society so that she could research it as much as she wanted, first hand! How

244

else could she have put it to use! How else? Ghost hunting with toys? Give me a fucking break!"

Edward was stunned. He looked at Deidra but could not catch her eye. The tears were too much. She was trying to catch her breath between the sobs that were now getting louder. "Okay. But how does it help you to kill her before you go?"

"Because she wants, more than anything, to go silently." Franklin stopped to smile. "Not in a blaze of glory, or in a big dramatic shoot out … just silently. Naturally. She wants to pass on to the next dimension. She is afraid to be stuck in this one and that fear is stronger than anything you can ever imagine. Why do you think she races so well? She's trying to live! She drives me crazy with her conflicted dare devil personality!"

"So you want to murder her."

"Yes. I'm taking what she took from me. A chance to pass on without trauma or stress. She'll be stuck here … or at least part of her will. I learned that from her."

Edward extended his arm further toward Franklin's face, keeping the gun aimed steady at him as he stood. "Then let's do this now."

Deidra looked at him sadly, her eyes swollen.

"Edward," Franklin said. "I need you to take over the races."

"No."

"Edward, please." Franklin's voice was desperate and hoarse. "I need you to do this for me—for the world. One day, you will understand. You were meant to take my place. I care about you so much," he spoke with tears in his eyes. "Your mother is so proud of you. You mean everything to her."

Edward shook uncontrollably as he raised the gun higher and into Franklin's face. He didn't want to hear him say another word. "I hate you for making me do this!" he yelled at him. "I don't want to do this!"

"I transferred all power over to you, Edward. Anthony knows what to do to prepare you. It's all taken care of. You are set for life."

Franklin shot Deidra and she collapsed instantly to the ground.

Edward screamed in disbelief. He had to find the power within him to keep from giving in to weakness. The thought of her death was overwhelming. He glanced at her body. Her arm was over her face with her sleeve folded back slightly. *No tattoos...*

Franklin opened his arms to his sides and stepped toward Edward. Edward shot him in the chest and face. He fell at Edward's feet. Edward stood frozen as he watched Franklin take his last breath. Franklin's blood was on his shoes. It shined in the light and made him want to vomit on himself, but he had to get out of there. He held his breath.

Without stopping to think about it any longer, Edward grabbed the computer from the desk and jumped over Franklin's body. He did his best to control himself. He could not look at her on the floor like that again. Not even a glimpse. He couldn't look because he knew it wasn't her. *I know there was part of a Rembrandt painting on that part of her arm...*

The door opened just before Edward could get to it and Deidra stuck her face inside the room to hiss at him, "Hurry up! We have to get out of here!"

"Jesus!" Edward said. It felt as if his heart had jumped into his throat. He had no time to let anything register in his mind. "How in the hell did you do that?"

"Were you crying over me?" Deidra joked as they jogged down the hallway to take the stairs.

"No, but I was about to. I wasn't sure what was going on. I just knew it wasn't you. I had a feeling it wasn't." Edward could hardly catch his breath.

"I told you the greys owed me. Because of Del Rio. Don't ever go there," she laughed. "Ever."

"Okay, okay," he smiled. "I won't."

33

Edward walked out of the bathroom and waited for her approval.

"I can't tell at all," she said. "You look fine."

He couldn't tell how sincere she was being, but had no choice in accepting her opinion. He did his best to wipe the blood from his shoes but his suit jacket was a mess. It was inside out and folded over his arm.

"The jacket has to go. Give me your gun and throw the jacket in the trash," she said while holding out her hand. "We need to board, like ... now."

Anthony had booked them first class tickets back to Dallas. After having $100,000 in cash delivered to a man in the Nevada desert named Sam, he worked to clear Deidra of all perceived betrayal because she had always helped him to conceal his own personal secrets. The club had always valued her anyway. She was an asset to them and her knowledge was beyond any material value. She was irreplaceable.

They needed to get back as soon as possible to catch up on some sleep. There would be a lot of meetings coming up, and Deidra was already preparing Edward's next phase of training in her head.

"I'm still going to boss you around," she smiled.

"I figured that part out, Deidra," he smiled in return as he followed at her heels to board their flight.

Deidra had already checked the Internet several times. The video was viral with the online conspiracy community. Many of the underground cyber activists' blogs were commenting on it and submitting links to it worldwide. They had dubbed it "The Alien Murder" video and "The Secret Military Alien Betrayal and Human Family Murder" video. Of course, Deidra didn't like the second title.

She let Edward sit by the window and stared at him until he was ready to notice.

"What?" he asked uncomfortably and with a large grin.

"We have a lot to do when we get back," she said while fluffing her hair.

It had been quite an experience walking through the airport with her. Even though they had been on the run, hunted, and almost murdered—she still looked amazing. Men rushed to open doors for her. Untraditional, tattooed, unashamed, and smoldering with attitude, she still had all eyes on her every move. He couldn't get used to her presence, as much as he tried, and still felt unworthy sitting next to her.

"We have to meet with our investors, explain what happened, and give them some sugar coated details about Franklin," she explained. "Then we have to plan the next race."

"Without the killing part," he suggested.

Deidra exaggerated a frown and rolled her eyes. "Well, I'm sorry, Eddie. But there are a lot of things you just don't understand. You were rushed into this life so quickly that you haven't had a thing explained to you yet about how important this race is in the order of things. The deaths happen, but it's not really bad. Like what you did to Franklin, it was like a gift in his case. You released him into *true* existence. Unfortunately for him though, it may not be a pretty one for a while." She stopped to study his face for a few seconds. "Things are not the way we have been taught. People exist in a very primitive physical state here. They are trapped until death."

"No. Deidra, killing is still wrong."

"I don't expect you to understand it or to understand the concepts completely. I don't expect you to see the art in it either

... or the fact that most of the people involved in the actual dying are criminals, mobsters, convicted felons ..."

"Death is not an art," he said, disgusted.

"Okay, you are not understanding what I mean," she sighed. "Franklin chose you and he must have seen the fragile soul within you. I'm sure he knew that you would bring some type of ... reform to our club."

"Reform is right. The killings, envelopes, taco stand stabbings ... all of that is going to stop."

"Hmmm," she replied. "I don't know if we can work around that completely but I have some great ideas to keep it exciting."

"So you think we can pull this off without gambling with death?" he asked.

"I don't know. Not entirely, but I think I have some ideas," she smiled. "Just remember, Eddie, that no matter how much you plan to tame things, the element of death must be a part of the race. It's what the aliens love best. And you just have a lot to learn about advanced alien civilizations to understand why."

Edward looked at her with a smirk. "They don't experience death the way we do."

"No, they don't. But with all of our differences, humans and aliens have figured out a way to trigger the door to an inter-dimensional space where emotions and memories exist like movies stuck in time." She moved in closer to him. "With the races we recreate a scene, a place in time, and spark it. We jump start emotions with it. Past and present emotions. Dressing up, the excitement of the cars, the risk of death ... the aliens feed off of it. And, sometimes we can communicate with the past memories of others when we do. Residual energy ... ghosts seem to manifest when scenes from the past are recreated or when a great deal of emotion is in the air."

"I don't understand," he said, hanging on her words.

"The races. They are a stage for the experiments. It's all very complicated. The aliens get to experience their favorite drug, human emotions, and we get to do paranormal research. We all win. There is a lot to explain. And you thought it was just a race."

"Experiments?"

"Oh, Eddie!" she gasped suddenly. "You are the leader of our club and you don't even know the name of it!"

"Yeah."

"Welcome to the most secret club on Earth," she said proudly and began waving at a stewardess for drinks. "The Secret Order for the Universal Study of the Afterlife Society." Deidra smiled when she saw the confused look on his face. "Or, The Afterlife Society ... for short."

"Afterlife?"

Deidra patted him on the knee and hoped to get a rum and coke as quickly as possible while Edward bit his lip. "I'm confused, because I thought this was about dealing with aliens, not ghosts," he said.

"Yeah, well, it's about both. Human emotions are like a drug on other planets. They love the whole drag racing thing, too. When we first set it up, we had no idea it would also spark evidence of the paranormal. Photos of the races and videos had all kinds of apparitions in them. Plus the whole thing makes millions of dollars. That's why Franklin wanted to set up some other racing deals with them. That's where the DNA labs come in. They need humans for their races—the ones they want to do on other planets."

Edward wanted to understand everything at once but couldn't. Every time he thought he had some part of it figured out, a secret bloomed into another secret.

"I told you nothing is what it seems, right?" she asked. "Always listen to me, Eddie. I'm always right."

Edward sat back in his seat and smiled.